PERILOUS PASSAGE

PERILOUS PASSAGE

Perilous Passage is an account of Terry Wilson's experiences, from the mid-1970s onwards, of the revolutionary Third Mind, originally developed by Brion Gysin, William Burroughs and their collaborators at the Beat Hotel circa 1959-1963.

The Third Mind is the creation of psychic symbiosis between two people in order to achieve a condition of revelatory consciousness, and liberation from ideological, moral and biological programming.

In *Perilous Passage* Terry Wilson describes the transformative shamanic system into which he was initiated by Brion Gysin, and the frought process of the continuation of the Third Mind which followed Gysin's death in 1986.

Terry Wilson's heretical history not only describes the application of Third Mind techniques, it is actually produced by them. His book questions the immutability of memory and the fixity of identity, and the integrity of the written word it is both a document of considerable importance, incarnating Third Mind strategies, and, necessarily, a fiction, "a story I am telling myself," "a deceit in the service of truth."

The book invokes Gysin's view of man as the "Bad Animal" the Third Mind is attacked by interested parties who want "to neutralise and assimilate a lifetime of psychic power into three-dimensional manipulative areas." *Perilous Passage* is a work of resistance, a mocking, splenetic attack upon all those who want to assimilate and destroy Gysin and Burroughs' great project of experimental consciousness.

Following Gysin's death, Wilson felt isolated and cut off, and *Perilous Passage* was a way out of loss and despair, a magical writing making contact possible with other initiates, other minds. Third Mind techniques, including cutting-up, systematic disorientation, out of the body experiences, and the use of drugs in the transformation of the self, are all evoked, but it is the search for psychic connection which is crucial defying the limitations of space and time, and cause and effect, disrupting the "control lines" operating within the psyche.

It is this radical and dangerous "opening" of consciousness which *Perilous Passage* explores, including the extension of the Third Mind beyond the limits of mortal existence, through the manifestations of "Brion Gysin," or "Bedaya," as Wilson calls his friend and teacher.

The confronting of psychic terrors, and the process of mourning and renewal which lies at the heart of the book, culminate in Wilson's description of his 2000 trip to Peru to take *ayahuasca* with the shaman Don Roberto, and his recognition of "a guided beginning to be a beginning," " to *be* non-being."

To read *Perilous Passage* is to be psychically transported — a unique example of the Third Mind in action.

Ian MacFadyen
2011

PERILOUS PASSAGE

The Nervous System and the Universe in Other Words

TERRY WILSON

SYNERGETIC PRESS
santa fe, new mexico, usa

Published by
SYNERGETIC PRESS
1 Bluebird Court
Santa Fe, NM 87508
www.synergeticpress.com

Copyright © 2012 by Terry Wilson.

All rights reserved. No part of this publication may be reproduced, stored in any retrieval system, or transmitted, in any form or by any means, electronic, mechanical, photocopying, recording, or otherwise without the prior permission of the publisher.

Second Edition

ISBN 978-0-907791-42-3 (alk. paper)

CONTENTS

Introduction i.
KA 1.

MAN FROM NOWHERE 9.

The Star St. Lazare Great Work (Creeps) An Old Hand We are Very Uncomfortable Here Playing for Time Fire We are Very Close The Man from Nowhere I am Here . . .?

CHATEAU ROUGE 67.

Return Ticket We are from Home I am Not Alone Displaced Persons Through the Fear Are You Inside Me?

THE NERVOUS SYSTEM 115.

The Flaw Changing the Cut-Outs The Darkness Curse The Call of Aural Beech All Rational Thought The Universe in Other Words

CREDITS

Cover photo by Ulrich Hillebrand.
Cover Design by Caponigro Design.

Lines by Paul Bowles on pages 68 and 83 from "Next to Nothing" and "Song" (*Next to Nothing: Collected Poems 1926–1977*, Black Sparrow Press, Santa Barbara, CA,1981).

Quotation on page 94 from a 1971 paper on hallucinogens by R. Gordon Wasson, quoted by Richard Yensen in "From Mysteries to Paradigms" (*ReVision*, Vol. 10, No. 4, Washington D.C., 1988).

The italicised quotations on pages 172, 173, 174, 175 are from the works of Charles Fort. (Revised editions, published by John Brown, London).

Opposite page illustration "The Universe, in Other Words" by Terry Wilson.
Dedication page Brion Gysin photo collage by Ira Cohen.
Page 5 Terry Wilson Montage by 3T Vakil.
Page 9 Terry Wilson, Ladbroke Gardens, Notting Hill, c. 1980, photos by Roberto Klein.
Page 67 Brion Gysin and Terry Wilson, leaving the Ritzy Cinema, Brixton, after Final Academy performances, 1982, by Ulrich Hillebrand.
Page 115 KJ's annual party. Brion Gysin, William Burroughs, James Kennedy McCann, Paris, early '80s, by Udo Breger.
Page 132 Mr Green (Murray Smith), by Trolley Bus (Bryan Mulvihill).
Page 178 People walking away, Hollywood Boulevard, 1965, by F.A. Wilson.
Page 180 "The Being-Wheel" by Terry Wilson.

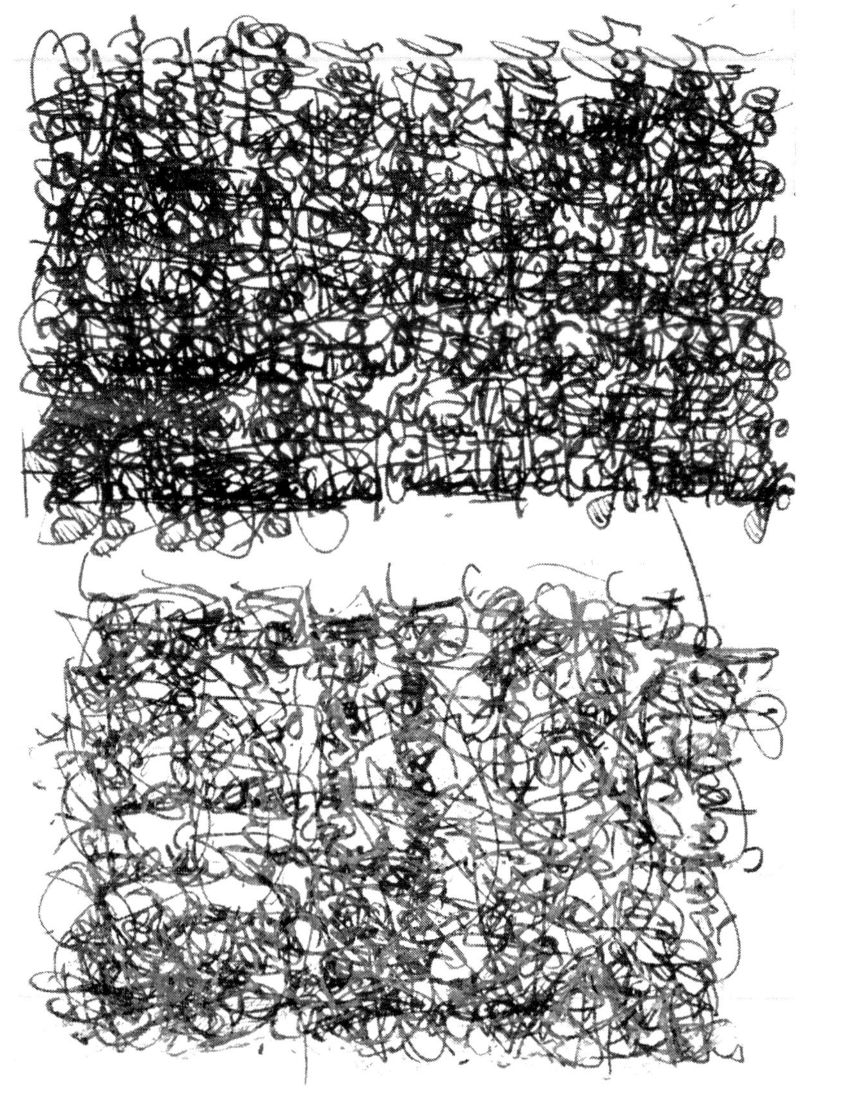

INTRODUCTION

Dreams of BG

"It is important to know that the world is held together by unresolved contradictions."
brion gysin

My books are an account of my apprenticeship under the tutelage of a master practitioner: Brion Gysin.

I had met him in 1971 and by '76, when we started work on *Here To Go*, "setting down first the voice of one and, then, the voice of the other" — I was, as I have written, an eager — *wanting* — volunteer on the shining path.

Brion, legendary "avant garde" maestro, peerless painter/writer-inventor/mentor was an accomplished shaman.

Perilous Passage finalises the *Green Base* trilogy which commenced with *Dreams of Green Base* and *'D' Train*. In these accounts I am not so much trying to detail a teaching method, a virtual impossibility in the case of the allusive and elusive "Massa Bedaya" (Brion resolutely refused to "teach," without ever ceasing to do so), but rather to describe the effects of what he called *the Process* on those concerned, most particularly myself. Brion did not confront people bluntly. The effect of his lessons, conversely, could be brutally blunt. Sink-or-swim blunt.

Here To Go completed, he set me up and left me with ever more complex tasks and situations, ranging from the menial to the quite literally unbelievable — (*Exercises* — "more fun and you need it") — and I have had to attempt — been compelled by his example to attempt — to tell a truth that, like Brion, transcends so-called fact. "A deceit in the service of truth" in the words of the Amazonian shaman Don Juan Tuesta (as quoted by Cesar Calvo, *The Three Halves of Ino Moxo*). "Fact" is right where you are now. Is it possible to bring a modicum of truth into such a situation? We'd all better hope so. I have worked principally from what are called dreams of an experience, rather than from the seeming occurrence, itself, as it were. Such is the Process. I'm not presenting what "really happened," "factually," because I don't know. In fact, I don't know if anything "really" happened at all. Do you?

"After all, what *is* a heart attack?" I remember him saying. "Does anybody really know?"

Trying to get at The Facts leads inevitably to The Fact that there are no such facts to get at.

I can say that in Paris in 1986 his body visibly became what it always had been: a strangely translucent shell.

Perilous Passage focuses for the most part on events as they developed just prior to and after Brion Gysin's death.

Ian MacFadyen has vividly described and commented on the general situation as presented herein in one of his insightful, rarely published essays . . .

"Phony magicians and phantom intelligence agents move in on rue St Martin, on the track of psychic power, while 'predatory hustlers' and 'bloodsuckers' emerge from under the floorboards, eager to grab a good-sized chunk of a dying artist's estate . . . [The apprentice's] initiation demands both risky out-of-the-body experiences and hazardous dealings with 'CREEPS', the con artists of a malign conspiracy . . . he has to continue Bedaya's teaching, a strategy known as the *Third Mind* . . . a system of psychic techniques for the electronic non-linear Space age, deconditioning practices which cannot be co-opted or media-ted by cultural and financial vested interests. Mutatis mutandis, the CREEP conspirators plan 'to take all that was seen to be useful out of Bedaya and dump the rest', including the 'unpredictable, unnecessary and unprofitable' concept of the Third Mind."

Having reached what at the time with astounding naivety given the precarious state of affairs appeared to be the culmination of this particular passage, both breakdown and breakthrough, the clinking together of two glasses of Irish coffee seemed to signify the arrival of a new age of revelatory collaboration. 'The Nervous System' indicates that this hope was soon dashed both by the disputive behaviour of the team of lost followers set up by Bedaya and the arrest and imprisonment of the manic KJ the Irish "cultural incendiarist" fabulist James Kennedy McCann (who had financed Brion through the last years of his life) on conspiracy charges, Dusseldorf, 1991. So, rather like the equally hapless Donner Party, we staggered onward, into the distinctly eerie and menacing realm of the "voice-distorted ventriloquist" known as Aural Beech.

MacFadyen concludes that:

"Some of the difficulties which Bedaya and Wilson — character and author, mentor and pupil — encounter in explaining the Third Mind are the result of the failure of critics to understand that this project is not artwork, personal expression or media intervention. It is something else entirely — an attitude of mind and a way of being in this world and other worlds which cannot be acquired, promoted or sold . . . the Third Mind is not another attack on the art market, one more crack at 'Deceptual Art,' or a psuedo-intellectual postmodernist scam on the French model — although its protagonists would be more than happy to promote such confusion and incomprehension.

"Bedaya may indeed, as Wilson says, have 'outmanoeuvred himself,' set up tactical confrontations and employed contradiction in ways which finally rebounded upon him. But then the chaos which surrounds his death, and the melancholy mixed with bitterness which accompany his dying are suitably Shakespearean elegies for a great *actor* — one who began as Hamlet and ended as Prospero. This is a way of saying that a chameleon life and the transformation of the self become theatrical and calculated in time . . .

"Art, like acting, requires subterfuge and tricks, professional artifice and cunning devices . . . forbidden acts of transgression which obliterate the distinction between the libertarian and the con man, the genius and the social Pariah. There is something appropriate in the ranks of crooks and charlatans swarming to Bedaya's deathbed: artists by any other name."

And *Perilous Passage* concludes with "The Universe In Other Words," an initiation into the mysteries of *ayahuasca* in Peru, where, as ever, the spirit of Bedaya presides, and where it finally became unavoidably obvious that all there really *is* is the peril of the passage on the other side.

Terry Wilson
2004

. . . and against all these considerations there was only the peril of the passage on the other side.

robert louis stevenson

The Master of Ballantrae

FOR BRION

Brahim John C.B.L. Gysin von-You-don't-know-who
Massa Bedaya

Also for

Norman Dark

Robert Potts

and George T. Harker,
inspirational teacher

With heartfelt thanks to Philippe Baumont and the late Murray Smith, both of whom provided essential material. And to Ian MacFadyen for unstinting assistance and encouragement.

KA

To begin at the beginning . . . give us a few statements about your background, school, etc.

Well . . . I grew up in the East End, post-war, working class environment; secondary school which I . . . er . . . never attended much after a while.

When did you first start to write? Why?

I've always written really . . . Up until my early teens I was much more into painting, sketching, but then I seemed to lose interest very suddenly, and I suppose really started writing at that time . . . adventure stories, that sort of thing. Then my parents took me to Australia, Adelaide, where we lived for two or three years and I got a job on a daily paper, first as copy boy then trainee journalist . . . flower shows, police courts, all the rest of it . . . a real pain . . . then we just sort of wound up back in England . . .

London?

Yeah, some rooms in Wembley, and . . . the Australian period had been very traumatic. I was in a rather shattered condition, not going out . . . and I started on *Dreams of Green Base* . . . 1965, thereabouts . . . I wasn't at all aware I was writing a book. I was in a strange, disconnected, almost catatonic state . . . and I was more or less simply recording dream experi-ence, a period of which I remember very little, thankfully.

It sounds, and reads, almost schizoid.

More than almost I think.

You then met William Burroughs and Brion Gysin.

About 1971, I had become dissatisfied with simply recording these experiences sequentially . . . I was totally lost with all this material really. Then on impulse I ordered *The Job* (Burroughs) and *The Process* (Gysin) from a local bookshop somehow knowing there was going to be revelation after revelation. I knew next to nothing about them. I'd read *Naked Lunch* a few years earlier and was really just sort of impressed and puzzled. I wasn't aware of it having any particular influence. Which it obviously did.

They obviously transformed what you were doing, eventually:

Yes. I had already cut into the text a bit and reordered separate paragraphs at random. So when I saw the possibilities opened up by the Cut Up technique, the implications, it really was a major revelation. Then, I somehow found Burroughs' phone number in London, Brion answered and said to come round sometime, if I wanted. So I met them like that. I showed up at Brion's door with some of Green Base ; he opened up, took the manuscript out of my hand and shut the door in my face . . . rather extraordinary meeting (laughs).

What exactly did you take from them?

Well I think they showed me a new way of thinking, of living. I would visit Burroughs when he was in London, and we'd talk . . . as far as *Green Base* was concerned, by 1975 I had what seemed at the time a great heap of manuscript it's not really all that long of course . . . I think at that time there were probably about three different, separate storylines in there, it was just everything I'd written over that period, and kind of juvenilia, much of it and I just reordered all the pages at random. It took about five, ten minutes? And that, more or less, was its final form; just a few pages that absolutely had to go back into their original sequence. I typed it out again just like that, all the stories cutting into each other. It was a book for boys, written by a boy . . . *

Does it bug you now to be identified with the Burroughs circus?

No . . . the 'circus', well you have to get the show on the road . . . and keep it there . . .

* The original subtitle of *Dreams of Green Base* (inadvertently omitted by the publisher) was '*The Ideal Book For Boys*'. LW

* * *

Was Here To Go *a hard book to write? Why did you want to do it?*

Well I've never known one that wasn't hard. Brion had barely survived a cancer operation in London and had moved back to Paris. I visited him there for the first time, at William's suggestion. I didn't know him well. He had never really lived in London, he was always on the move, back and forth; he'd still kept his apartment in Tangier during that London period . . . it just seemed at the time that Brion was never going to write anymore, and, after *Green Base,* I felt pretty much the same . . . So I thought, if he can't write it, he can say it . . . the point about *Here To Go* was that neither of us had to write it, in the usual sense. It was a case of bringing in the tape recorder and getting him to talk . . . So we worked away at it for a few years. I liked to think of it as a book by him, he liked to think of it as a book by me . . .

I'd say that for me, paraphrasing Brion, a good many things were discovered or rediscovered or made more evident during that period . . . and eventually came another sort of collaboration . . .

Another extraordinary meeting?

As described in *'D' Train*, yes.

The aspect Burroughs picked up on straight away in his notes for 'D' Train *was the* 'Ka'. *Do you agree with Castaneda's idea that each person's* 'Ka' *is of the same sex?*

There's an ancient Egyptian text called *A Dialogue of the Dispute Between the Man and His Ka* . . . I think perhaps in this case the term *Ba** is used . . . but anyway that could almost be a subtitle for *'D' Train*. The *Ba* for them was something like the actual embodiment of the *Ka* **, which is more or less one's parallel being, spiritual double, and is of the same sex as the person concerned which Burroughs is also at pains to emphasize in his notes

* *The Report About the Dispute of a Man with his Ba, Papyrus Berlin 3024* (John Hopkins Press, Baltimore, 1970)

** Or vice versa, as the case might be. Burroughs related the *Ka* to the non-dominant brain hemisphere.

D TRAIN routes the reader though the Land of the Dead. In this perilous passage, the only one a man can trust, the only one who can guide him through the Land of the Dead, is his KA, his Psychic Double. And the Ka needs the man as much as the man needs his Ka. A tragic impasse blocks all but a very few from the Ka. It isn't foregone like salvation. It's a desperate -- - (Terry may fill in a word or two here.) D TRAIN is a book concerned with spiritual basics. Young boys need it special. They may even listen.

William Burroughs.

William Burroughs' original 'D' Train *Cover Notes, 1985.*

What is the significance of gay sexuality in all of this?

Here we have this existence in which we're disconnected from the *Ka*, hungry earthbound ghosts, partial beings . . . and all these people hungrily and endlessly searching for intimate contact with their own sex, apparently propelled by simple sexual desire. Well of course it's not that simple at all. But it would seem obvious that what we're describing here, all this endless searching from person to person is the search for the *Ka*.

* * *

In *Green Base* really you have the situation of the disembodied earthbound spirit, totally disconnected. *'D' Train* describes the situation once the parallel beings have come together. That's it, more or less. That's where the *'Dispute'* comes in. A kind of inexplicable area of often total conflict. They've been divided into separate bodies, separate egos, powerful forces working against them . . . and to quite an extent of course both of them would like to deny all this and retreat back into some kind of peace . . . like back into the womb, for instance . . . the ever open door . . . and around and around the whole thing goes . . .

* * *

You invariably have the sense of working with the material word. You cut it up, disembody, decontextualise. What sort of effect are you after? Is there any sort of tradition involved?

Hmmm . . . Brion described *'D' Train* as a journey 'through a long night of the soul past Danger and Despair to come in ultimate Delight' . . . hopefully . . . the Delight often seems a long time coming! But I think that would actually be a good description of both *Green Base* and *'D' Train.* Initially one is simply trying to affect a change in one's own consciousness of course. As to there being any kind of tradition involved, I'd say it was a tradition of transmission, which operates in very specific circumstances . . . collaboration. 'The *Ka* needs the man as much as the man needs the *Ka* . . .'

Certainly Dreams of Green Base *and* 'D' Train *read like the autobiography of a spirit. Has it now become a problem? Have you burned down your psychic past?*

I think they are the autobiography of a spirit, and it is and always has been a problem. Burning down my psychic past? To an extent perhaps, an extent.

* * *

Any plans now for the future? Do you foresee a radical change of direction?

Well . . . I would say there's nothing to do but to keep on doing it.*

* Extracted from *KA: An Interview with Terry Wilson* by David Darby (Inkblot Publications, Oakland, CA., 1986).

The standardised explanation was published.
I shall oppose it with heresy. Throughout this book,
I shall say that all expressions of mine are only mental phenomena,
and sometimes may be rather awful specimens, even at that.
But, if we examine our opposition, and find it wanting,
and if my own expression includes much that is left out,
my own expression is not wanting,
whether it's wanted, or not.

charles fort

MAN FROM NOWHERE

THE STAR

A distant time, young man typing.

In his room he remembers the perilous passage.

Two candles are lighting the room one creating a bridge to the other, many persons are crossing it their own way from the bed to the chair, the only chair of the room, a kind of seventies plastic chair . . . We were both waiting for it to be more strong we like that very much it's not too expensive for the price to pay even though you always pay it very much , honestly you could make it more precious if you like delicate spirit, wild as it can be . . .

Returning to the story we don't exactly remember what it was, knowing that it can be everything we decide to wait for it to be a little stronger and a thing suddenly happened the window breaks and the wind is creating a bridge to the other. There it was a bridge from the bed to the chair. A door open. We were waiting for the candles. We entered the room . . . A bare empty room with skylight, irradiated . . . a single star, hovering . . .

I love courage when you want to stay even though you always disappear trying to find what we have . . .

He sits back from the typewriter.

In a corner of the room I am claiming "I am speechless . . . you better write my book for me. I can arrange a contract for you."

I looked into the mirror. A misty scene.

A policeman typing our answers.

"When did you see that star?"

"At night."

"What time was it?"

"Not yours."

"What did it look like?"

"Like a world burning in the sky."

The world imagination, the torrent of worlds about him, the great gallery of power, a moral sting fluttering in the night . . .

Lost do we know when? Each time you are you feel it now. Fraternity. Personally it doesn't help the spiritual double . . . delicate spirits wild as they come, both waiting for it to be more strong. And many are crossing it the land of this perilous passage two candles are lighting the way. Knowing that it can be everything we decide to do what you want. I hate to wait for it to be stronger, a supermarket in my nerves returning to the story we don't remember exactly. Through the Land of the Dead that long long way we have known and known so well . . . pay for it very much . . .

Our lesson will be to arrive where we started this magic melts slowly in us again.

I am speechless. You better write. In the sky . . .

Are you sleeping? No. I am kind of floating . . .

Spin out my distant story, out to a distant star . . . There is no time . . .

ST LAZARE

"Hmm. It would be you."

"You were expecting me."

"Not exactly this minute,"

"I have a tendency to show up like this."

"Hmm. Like an incubus." I frowned.

"Do you have any idea what it is you're doing?"

"Aren't you going to tell me?"

"You've been here before . . . ?"

"Yes . . ." As I sit here smoking I remember it . . .

St Lazare is empty, barren where lifelessness lies the mirror is alternately radiant and dead . . . where the relics lie I still recall, when the spirit's lost and the mighty fall . . . The Land of the Dead, created by YSL certainly . . . lifelessness lies exotic, radiant and dead. Radiant lifelessness. The sun.

I stirred my coffee listlessly.

"You seem to have managed a total fuckup."

I shrugged. "Appearances can be deceptive."

"We are so short of *people* . . ."

"Uh . . ."

"People are leaving us faster than they're coming in."

"Feet first, quite often . . ."

"All they have to do is remember what was forgotten or dissociated or inactivated . . . So the Old Man and I drew in the nets . . ."

"Hmm . . . bring on the frightened ones . . ." I smiled. "Well, they have other commitments."

"That's what they think."

"I think, in the words of our ellusive colleague, it's a case of trying to give bones to jellyfish."

"Then it would be better to choose somebody with bones in the first place."

"You're talking about another *person*."

"You're the one who brought fish into the discussion."

I sighed.

"I presume there's some reason we have to be sitting here freezing to death."

"That's what we're talking about."

I shivered.

"Basically I'm cold. I want to get warm."

"What do you want?"

"I want out."

"And you want it to be as easy as that!" he snapped his fingers.

"Easy or hard . . ."

I paused.

"I'd just like to take a long holiday . . . a long trip and just see what happens."

"But don't you understand, that's what you did. And you're seeing it . . ."

London is spinning.

Mosaics explode on the wall. The fire. The flickering room, breathing, heaving.

"These are the lost days before the future. This is the past between mosaics . . ."

3 Brandon Grove, 68 Orchard Lane, 58 Chapel Road, 23 Princes Square, 135 rue St Martin, 1 Queensborough Terrace, rue Montmartre, 10 Ladbroke Gardens, 18 Lancaster Road flash by

These are the lost days before the rue de l'Assomption, this is 9 rue St Lazare flashes by we shall not cease

I walked home, shivering, sweating profusely, wind whipping into me . . . time, horribly cold.

I remember we were together in a dark expanse of woodland. At night. Scattered ruins of buildings once grand. We sat and talked. Bedaya was there. He approached to talk, giving you a strange pointed glance and you stepped back through the door.

"That was a rather sharp look" I said.

He assured me that everything would be okay . . ."As long as you have the strength to survive this initiation . . ." I realised he didn't want you to hear this. Step back through the door.

"I'm sure everything will be okay"I said. He looked concerned.

The great noise from outside. I opened the door and a horde of costumed attackers swarmed forward slammed the door in their face and we all ran a great number of us piling down a ruined staircase once ornate and I knew you had disappeared again.

We pushed down into unconsciousness.

I awake lying on cold hard boards like the prow of a ship wet and naked all the bells in the house are ringing

The police are at the door!

I cower at the corner of the window staring down at them can they see me in the dark? They give the bell another push then slowly walk across the road to the car, hesitate, looking back at the house, staring down at them can they see down into unconsciousness?

They drive away.

The loneliness. The infinite loneliness. Totally alone, disconnected and frightened we answer each other's bodies.

But beyond the pain and the death does lie,
The heart that never once did lie.

A long dark road to the *Ka*, hesitate, looking back, scattered ruins of buildings once grand you have disappeared again.

And I knew we were all spirits on the road, and it's hard to write such things as occurred . . .

I'd made it easily through customs and found a cab.

"Is that any use to you?"

The man pushed the *Sunday Times Magazine* across the table.

"Thanks" I said as he got up and left.

Tucked away inside there was an envelope containing Swiss francs to the tune of about £700. Expenses.

I was booked into a rathole on rue Montmartre . . .

"You have a Great Werke in front of you."

"Yes?" I laughed. *"What is it?"*

"To catch a soul . . . And the Blue Virgin will move in on you."

"Who is she?"

"What a question . . . !"

A knock at the door. I opened up and Madame was blasting French at me a mile a minute. A telephone call.

"You're there."

"Uh-huh."

"Well, take it easy . . . You've got enough."

"Sure."

"Okay."

"The very fact of being born, means we have nothing to lose."

"Or everything . . ."

"People, if they think at all, think we are engaged in some kind of chess game in which we win or lose power and control in the world. That is not the case . . ."

"Everything you say can be reversed" I said.

"Well, then that's not necessarily the case."

"*All right.*" I smiled.

I lay back listening to the traffic roar. I had not realised it was morning.

(CREEPS)

"Be as cautious as you can, of course, for you know that as soon as you have anything like a kingdom, enchanters and conjurors will always drop in from all over Creation to take it away from you, naturally enough . . ."*

And they come in all shapes sizes and sexes . . . the absolute *pain* who showed up imploring, pleading, threatening at my door in the Princes Square Hotel, her mysterious "brother" hovering behind in the darkness . . ."You must do our bidding" . . . or the hatchetfaced bombed-out creep who was suddenly accusing me of raping his wife across the length of a crowded restaurant . . . I sat back, blank faced, everybody in the place staring at me . . . Is this real? . . . I had previously opened a newspaper and there was the story of a Los Angeles multiple rapist apprehended in a hospital after one of his intended victims had bitten off one of his fingers. His name? Mine of course. Returning home trying to open or close my umbrella one of the spokes broke off and went right through the tip of my finger . . . and now right here on cue is this jerk loudly accusing me of defiling his precious piece of ass, which by the look of him is more than he ever got around to doing, a frantic closet . . . Later, calming down, he is convinced he's made a mistake . . ."but many times on the street my wife pointed you out to me as the person who did it . . . Why would she do that to me?" he whines. To *him*? Well, why indeed.

Not to mention the sententious shaven headed old bore who appeared out of nowhere sitting down at my table in a bar intoning portentously: "You have no more than twelve years to live." He can tell by my fingers. But he can help me, no doubt about it . . .

Or, if all else fails, bring on the Blue Virgin . . .

"And a thing suddenly happened suddenly the window broke and the wind enters the room destroying everything in its passage in five seconds the

*Brion Gysin, *The Process*

whole house explodes and crashes to the ground — a virgin appears with all her staff dressed in blue costume created by YSL certainly — there is a supermarket in my nerves —"

(The whole building starts to explode along with home somewhere around here).

This one is a real lulu, and sticks like glue.

One day the Blue Virgin appears at your door with a huge empty canvas . . . empty . . . a lot of space on that canvas, which represents your apartment of course . . . but she is going to fill it up pretty soon, never fear . . . softly softly, nothing heavy yet, no threats — understanding . . . and slowly, just a little every day — (This is very important. If anyone just came in and saw the godawful thing right there in front of them they'd immediately see what it represented) — the canvas is coming alive, in your room — which is also getting just a little bit less empty every day — filling up with more and more writhing voodoo goddesses — and she's got you. She is HOME.

Yes, they are coming down off the wall to shake your hand.

Well, nothing to do except bring things to a head, cut your losses and set about enhancing your position . . . or whatever left of it hasn't been siphoned off by the Blue Virgin.

Now, who are these . . . people?

Who knows? Enchanters? Conjurors? Usually not. Mostly they are not very enchanting, to me at least. They certainly wouldn't bother trying the Blue Virgin on me. Take it away, lady, and don't bother to bring it back. It's obvious that most of them, being naturally ill-intentioned or at least terribly *wanting* — the two have a tendency to go together — are simply dupes who are controlled.

Controlled by — ?

Some power wants to keep us right *here*, right where we are. Because this power simply couldn't exist if we were anywhere else.

Another call. "Hi! It's George!"

"Good God!" I muttered.

"Uh? . . . I'm in Paris and I just got your number." He was nearby.

"Well ... " I paused. I wanted to know *how* he got my number.

"There's a café on the corner here. I'll see you there." I gave him the address. He said he'd come immediately.

"Yeah" I mumbled.

George was about twenty-two, so he said. A big fat heavy balding moon-faced prana pincher who claimed to be a writer, dressed in regulation black stormtrooper chic, ski cap, windcheater, jeans and boots, chronically creating a creepily unpleasant atmosphere of resentment, insinuation, slyness and desperate need, George couldn't be chic to save his life but he could certainly be oppressive.

He came in and sat down at my table.

"Take a seat" I said, smiling. "How did you get my number?"

"Oh, some guy phoned after I arrived and said you were here, I didn't understand who he was He just left your number . . ."

Was he lying?

"Well, and what can I do for you, George?"

He started back in his seat giving me his nervous, insecure little boy smile of mock amusement.

"I just came to say hullo."

"Well . . . *Hi,* George!"

He turned around and ordered a coffee.

I had been acquainted with George in London for the past few months. Again, someone had given him my number. His technique was to remain firmly seated fixing the other with his baneful imploring gaze while consuming endless coffee and cigarettes, never rising until the other did. He stuck like a limpit.

"Jesus!" I thought. "I should've asked him about the number over the phone . . . but, maybe . . ."

Maybe he was just playing dumb. No, I decided, it was too real. But he could play dumber than he actually was. Where did he fit into this?

George was complaining that life was hard.

"Where did it say it was going to be easy?" I replied

He was ordering another coffee.

"I have a few things to do" I said, got up and left.

Walking off I felt sure George was making another phone call back in the cafe.

I found another place and sat down, feeling somewhat vexed. George didn't fit into this, or anything at all, except as nuisance value, something he was certainly well suited for . . . You could be taking a drink in a bar in Tennant Creek or someplace, and in would walk George, looking surprised.

"If you can't get some character like that off your back . . ."

"He's not on my back, but he's practically everywhere else I happen to be . . . much too often."

"Well do something about it . . ."

But I didn't see very much more of George.

I could hardly drag myself down into the cab and almost blacked out. A feeling of utter doom.

He was slapping my face.

"Where are you?"

I opened my eyes and looked out at something that at first looked like Byzantium, rain streaming down the window in all its glory. He reached across and wound the window down on a grand apartment block and I knew it was the rue de l'Assomption swaying and shivering in front of me

"Yeah, I've lived here" I said without turning my gaze fixed frozen as the great glass door suddenly exploded — a great white hole — *"Keep looking!"* — a great white

I woke up to a smell of dried vomit and ripped off my shirt before there was any recurrence. There was a note on the table telling me I was expected at 2 PM on the Quai someplace. I fell back onto the bed.

OOOOOOOOOOAAAAAAAAAAAIIIIIIIIIIIIIIIIIIIIIII!

I was walking down the steps at about two when there was this awful seal-like roar, a great thrashing — and George was emerging from the river, fully clothed, still wearing his hat! I stood amazed. He looked like a huge stricken sea cow.

"Well, you look kinda upset!" I said, unable to stop myself.

He lumbered forward a few steps tried to croak something and then threw up a good deal of the Seine. He stared down at it amazed and then looked up at me. His eyes were huge.

I stepped back cautiously but his gaze went back down to the vomit.

I sat down on a bench staring at him.

"What happened?" I asked.

"I was walking along here" he spluttered, gesturing around, " . . . and somebody just came from behind   and pushed me *in*!"

"Did you see this person?"

"I was . . . looking at the river and then . . ." His voice trailed off.

"Well you'd better get a cab and get home before you get pneumonia" I said.

"I haven't got the *money* for a cab!" he yelled. His big eyes were glaring at me out of his man-in-the-moom face.

"There's a metro very close" I offered. "Do you need a ticket?"

His head dropped again and for a second I thought he was about to charge, but he abruptly whirled around to face the river then back to me and then swept off wildly sloshing his way up the steps to the boulevard.

I sat back smiling to myself and left after a few minutes.

AN OLD HAND

"Seen anything of this . . . George, recently?"

"No, not much . . . I think he caught a cold."

"I daresay." A faint trace of a smile. "And how are you?"

"I figure I could make it through to the end of the week at least."

"You recognised that street yesterday."

"Yes. But it was all so fast . . . the door . . . that's all I remember . . ."

"There's a lot more to it than that."

"The door exploded, or imploded, or whatever . . . I was dying . . ."

"Yes . . ."

The ashtray was moving across the table without any apparent assistance. I was staring at it. He was staring at me.

The street yesterday, when did I ever live there? Did I ever live there? Why did I say that?

"You have no memories after that . . . ?"

" . . . I was down on the street . . . on my hands and knees . . . crying for help, but no one could see or hear me . . ."

"Dying."

"Yes."

It was the cafe terrace. It was crowded. Frighteningly old, congealed, they had all learned from their mistakes . . . old people muttering elegant boulevards.

"Mistakes are deadly."

"You'll have to meet a Mr Green . . . Murray Green."

"And who is Mr Green?"

"I'd like you to find out . . ."

I stared at the floor. It was sparkling.

"It seems that . . . George, was a ploy to engage your attention . . . Mr Green has been hovering for quite awhile . . ."

"Hmmm . . ." I frowned. "An old hand, uh?"

"Yes, he's a bit long in the tooth."

The bar in Pigalle I frequented looked and sounded like a demented parrot house.

In London it would have been excruciating. In Paris it was excruciating, no doubt, but I didn't care too much. I settled down.

I was staring at the wall. It looked like it had been designed by Berard when he was down to the dross. Pretty good, in fact, I smiled. I looked around again.

The conversation was louder with every drink. Just in front of me a dapper, willowy old gentleman, suit, tie, cane, raincoat draped over an arm, was trying to make himself heard. He was asking if a seat was available. He was addressing the unresponsive occupants of the next table but his left pupil was glittering in my direction. At least seventy years old, hook nosed and hairless, he looked like some kind of cross between a buzzard and a piranha.

"Take a seat, Mr Green" I called out.

He made a half turn towards me then gasped as if in ecstacy. He drifted languidly over.

"You recognized me!" he gushed. "And I *you*!"

"You've seen my photograph" I smiled.

He simpered. "Yes, I have. I've been following your career."

"Yes?"

"You don't live in Paris?"

"No. Holiday."

"Ah yes. But I wonder if Paris is such a good idea. It's delightful of course . . . but one needs open space, and quiet . . ."

"I'm sorry, I can't hear you."

"Quiet!" he yelled.

"Oh, quiet . . ."

"Yes, I think that's what you need   a break. Pack a bag and set off . . if you have the money . . ."

"I could sell my stamp collection."

He ignored this. "Oh yes, that's the thing to do . . ." he said firmly.

"I have some very rare items."

He frowned. His eyes were ice cold, watery . . ."Yes, yes . . . I think that's what you have to do . . ."

He rose abruptly and nimbly.

"Au revoir, Mr Green" I said.

A corner of his mouth twisted down into something like a smile.

"British Intelligence seems to be suggesting I take a holiday," I said.

"More or less . . . What do you think about it?"

I shrugged. "Dump him in the river."

"Hmmm. I think not . . . I mean, after accepting so much of their money . . ."

His face was expressionless. My mouth was suddenly very dry.

"They got to me before you did . . ."

"Yes. I didn't see the point in giving you any more . . ."

"Jesus!"

For one mad moment I felt like hitting him. He was watching me closely.

"Well, I wouldn't want to do anything stupid, and spoil your enjoyment of all this" I said rather loudly.

"You mean even more stupid?"

"Don't give me that shit. You set me up."

"Hmm. So smart."

I didn't necessarily believe him anyway.

"Listen, you know that time and circumstance will obliterate everything we say. You're playing these games and I'm afraid that irreperable damage has been done . . . Don't you think that if you put me in the picture things might be a little easier . . . ?" My voice trailed off.

"No . . ."

I sat down suddenly on a park bench. I was trying to remember something.

I was a child walking into a restaurant with two people I knew to be my parents. I looked straight ahead and I could see no further than about ten feet. Beyond that was just a fog. There was nothing beyond that. I was a child walking.

We took a table, artificial hands were forking food into my mouth, I couldn't taste it. I seemed to be looking through a telescope, how far away I couldn't say there was a man watching me. He was staring. And my gaze was fixed on him also.

There was nothing beyond that. So it seemed.

"They were not *my* parents, but they were quite familiar to me, as parents . . ."

"Yes, they were not your parents, but other parents. And who was the child?"

"It seemed to be me."

"Yes, it seemed to be you . . ."

"It wasn't?"

"The man you were looking at was you."

"Quite a trick."

"But the same thing happened to you as a child . . . You simply chose to see it through the eyes of another."

"Look —"

"That's enough for now . . . You have about as much strength as Philip . . ."

He was staring into my eyes.

"My cat . . . just a few months old . . ."

My head dropped to my knees. It jerked back up and there was an old man staring at me with genuine concern.

"*Monsieur?*" He took a hesitant step forward.

"*Ca va, ca va*" I mumbled, dazed.

There was a grafitti scratched onto the bench:

on est tres mal ici.

I was blasted out of a deep sleep. Mr Green's voice.

"Hullo, dear boy, how are you?"

"I have lost my gun and nothing to eat and Indians hunting me."

He laughed. "Oh dear . . . Yes, yes, it's a holiday you need . . . just get away" he stated flatly.

I agreed with him.

"I've been reading your book" he continued. "That passage at the beginning where that creature comes into your room . . . and I suddenly had the absurd fantasy that she would come back again . . . you are both there in your room and there she is outside down on her knees picking the lock moaning: "*I miss him so much!*" . . . You know, I can just see it, can't you?"

"Yes, I can just see it."

"You see, it's a question of background. A creature like that has a background which is nothing but frustration and repression. Nobody wanted her. So there is nothing she can do in life but use all the slyness and cleverness she has at her disposal. And she has a lot. And then she is very dangerous."

"And in such a case how could I get her off my back, Mr Green?"

"Ah-*hah*!" he cackled, then said he absolutely had to hang up and to please call him Murray.

I took tea at Mr Green's apartment.

He was in a thoughtful mood.

"Your books, what do you see as the purpose of writing them."

"To make some money . . . it's therapeutic."

I was getting used to needling Mr Green.

"Yes . . ." He laughed. "But you want to have some effect on the minds of your readers."

"Sure . . . the current situation is most severe, to say the least . . . To try and change it a little . . . or a lot."

"You want to save the world!" He moaned, wearily.

"No, not at all! But I think you do . . . You're playing for Time, Mr Green."

"Dummies, fodder . . . and you want to save them . . . ! That's absurd . . . as if anything could . . . they are *fodder*!" His mouth quivered into a thin grimace. "It's unfortunate . . ." He didn't look as if he thought it was unfortunate.

"But they are essential, aren't they, to keep everything *right here*, right here where it always has been . . . all these dummies, with a few select ventriloquists . . . ?"

Mr Green smiled. He was staring deeply into his Earl Grey, as if consulting an oracle.

"Where it has always been" he repeated, both definitively and ironically.

He sighed slightly.

"I think you're misguided, dear boy . . . The situation is only severe if you insist on making it so. I think you have made your point. Now let it go. There is nothing to be *gained* that way . . . other than the fate of Joan of Arc, if that's what interests you . . ."

I said nothing.

"Oh come on, let it go! Why suffer? We all hope for other places . . . There are other places . . . I'm sure everything will be taken care of. You've made your *point!*"

As I walked back clouds were making room for the sun and the air was suddenly like spring, an exhilarating thinness . . . the sun, remember it . . . ?

That first meeting, there, years ago . . .

"A Great Werke . . ."

Why was I in Paris   and when? I didn't know which time it was and was almost beyond caring.

"The same thing happened to you as a child . . ."

Yes . . . I'd been sick, glandular fever . . . it was my first day out . . . the scene was just a dancing haze of patterns . . . someone sat down and started talking . . ." He wasn't talking to any body in particular, just an interception of the light . . ."

"To catch a soul . .."

And later: "The training you will receive here will be absolutely essential to your survival in the near future. All activities are of the utmost significance. All is crucial . . ."

A great white *flash*

Was that a memory or just a fiction I concocted? Everything is pretty much dreamland until the first orgasm snaps you out of it and you are in the land of hunters and the hunted . . .

Firstly there are the parents. And, before that, the Book of the Dead would say, we encounter the Others   in every direction a pair of people engaged in intimate physical contact   fucking. And, feeling the infinite desire for another here we fall completely under the control of these fucking people . . . there they are, down on the carpet by the sofa, fire on . . . children are good for The Place. Bring on the Christmas decorations. . . the little lord Jesus lays down his sweet head feeling the infinite desire for another, all over the world . . . physical contact. Child of the dead. There they are, the Others   in every direction

(Children avoid them, stepping over them . . . all over the world . . .)

A long dark road . . . Entrapped. Earthbound . . . permanent crisis.

If I'd eaten today I feel certain I'd've thrown it all up . . .

Into oblivion. It takes everything I've got to get out of the room. Then there's the question of getting back.

To where?

a postcard on the desk in front of me.

Your delay awful. Hope you can make it soon.

Please take care

Did I write that?

Why do I never see any other clients in this hotel? Madame comes over as nice enough but is prone to take me for the odd 200 fr. occasionally. Well, she knows how long I've been here and God knows I am lacking in worldly context . . . Just as long as she gets paid . . .

Another call from Mr Green.

"My dear! I'm so glad to hear your voice! I had the premonition that you were *dying*. I'm so relieved . . ."

I thanked him.

"Well . . . you're all right . . ."

"I'm going to have to buy a spray . . . The room is infested with huge flies."

"How positively parochial!"

"Did you know Ivor Powell?" I suggested abruptly. "A friend of Gerald Hamilton . . ."

"No . .. " His voice had a definite edge to it. "Wasn't he an . . . agent ."

"Yes, he was."

(Ivor Powell was a practising clairvoyant, amongst other things, sometimes known as Omar. "Ex-" Intelligence. Gerald Hamilton is sufficiently well known. Isherwood's Mr Norris. Both dead now.)

Mr Green hadn't very much time left.

But, in the midst of all this, we had established the foundation for the continuance of the Third Mind.

So we were subjected to threats and support from all manner of interested parties.

Time healed the awful delay and killed Bedaya.

"No more extra time."

Finally into the Fire.

PLAYING FOR TIME

(YOU HEAR ME NOW???)

The delay was that long blank period I've been describing. And yet we had fought our way through. To a breathtaking view of existence. Survived a shattering onslaught.

Who do these people like Mr Green represent?

Well, they are simply agents, double agents . . . At least . . . Do they themselves have any real idea as to who or what they're actually representing? I don't know. I think they must have some idea. Personally I find Mr Green quite charming, you're in the presence of a charming, intelligent person, beautiful manners in the old style . . . An adventurer in the old sense of the word. Low friends in high places . . .

As far as he's concerned, right *here* is where his pickings are. And his pickings are the beings trapped here. A predatory parasitic organism. He doesn't want anyone to get out from under. He doesn't see the point. They're where they should be. Why try to *spoil* things?

But with Mr Green, he was obviously taking a very personal interest. Which indicates that his superiors . . . — or *Time* — was putting him on the spot. He was nearly eighty. That type of agent frequently ends completely washed up, destitute. Nobody will touch him anymore. Probably the CIA, the vulgar mechanized peasants, had not even heard of him. It was too late. He'd been given his assignment. If we got *out* — *he* wouldn't. He had no time.

Operation Blue Virgin was in full swing.

The Blue Virgin, of course, can be found weeping rivers of holy tears at select grovelling spots throughout the world, often aided by rudimentary machinery in back. Mother at Home, her agents abroad are many.

Some are naturals.

The old gypsy queen drags her bags of sacred junk along the boulevard, thin as a broomstick under the bangles, spangles and layers of rotting robes courtesy of the dirt-and-grime-of-centuries department back at the penthouse.

(Could be the Duchess of Wind out on the job . . . Mr Green's mouth twists into a thin grimace . . .)

She stops dead. She is staring through the window of a ratty draperie, staring at the assistant, a girl neither young nor old, seeing the years of frustration and repression, the slyness, the vulnerability in the curious blank face. A natural.

She enters the shop.

It is done very quickly. She gives instructions, paints a representation of the evil eye on the girl's hand, she must take this to the apartment on rue St Lazare and then wash it off at a certain time, not too inconspicuously . . . and all is done as I have told . . .

Already the huge empty canvas has entered the apartment to be worked on by this medium, evil eyes in every direction, spilling out into the room, spilling the voodoo colours.

Time squirms out of the canvas . . . bugs, mice . . .

My mind felt suddenly very clear and I saw Bedaya sitting at his table, his face blurred, fuzzy like an old Comte . . . the unmistakable voice . . .

"What, you never heard of her contact with the sort of people who later became the CIA? She had gone into trance and located the captain of the British dirigible the R-101 . . .

"The dirigible is on fire, we are going down!"

"And indeed the R-101 *did* crash . . . all the fault of those contractors just typical of her, she was always trying to make the Air Ministry . . . daily 24-hour-a-day game next day the news came that it had crashed naturally being one up on your psychic opponent someplace between Belgium and France . . .

"I have denoted a crossroads to do something absolutely *terrible*!"

"She'd done her trick and made her effect."

"She went before the Psychic Ten about this and she'd cleared her name, she'd gone to Vienna where her extrapersonalities immediately took one sweeping glance at my bare knees and my kilt . . . and asked the usual questions . . . She had those spirit guides one of which was a 16th century charming young man in skirts, Persian at the court of Shah Jehan or something."

"Couldn't you both come round to dinner . . . ?"

I saw her through his eyes, staring intently . . .

"During your Japanese translation work at the receiving and transmitting centre you saw those documents . . . Pearl Harbor, Hiroshima . . . did you translate that message traffic? *Where* are your copies? *What* are your intentions? You *cannot* rewrite or blackmail history . . ..."

And his voice faded, spilling sun and french windows out of the room spilling the colour of roses down on the stone garden of an empty canvas, early morning, and I am in the garden of a charming country house, up against the crumbling brick wall, shielded from the sun and french windows of the house by an arch of roses down on the stone making love to a spirit form I am conjuring kissing the body my head between the legs the soft hair of the thighs caressing my face . . . until the figure disappeared . . . (it was you).

I walked back to the house dressed only in a blanket wrapped around me to the entrance there was mail by the door several packages I looked at them urgently difficult to see, nothing for me, there was a note saying all mail will be delivered directly to the guest rooms.

Into the house holding onto my blanket. Facility, Duchess of Wind was there and reminding me that this young Arab disciple is arriving any minute and in he walked, unattractive very slippery dishonest face. She took over and we were seating ourselves on cushions him bringing out a tape recorder and the rest of his equipment as if we'd arranged for an interview. Well, she probably had. I felt uncomfortable my blanket kept slipping off he was having trouble with his equipment . . .

The Duchess was talking in hushed tones in Arabic with some other visitors, apparently about him, we were all seated on cushions on the floor, inside in whispers. She turned to me —

"I see what you mean about disciples" then she is saying something like "I first met Matilda through Mata Hari "

The Arabs were all sharply dressed in expensive silk suits, jewellery, thin moustaches, kinky black hair receeding, one got up and presented me with a large packet, obviously containing clothing. He was most impressed with me when we met, he was not so sure in the car later, but now everything is fine, I am most profound. I thanked him and took the package. Inside was a beautiful grey-brown djellabah-like duffel coat, he was telling me about the material — "It is not exactly wool" I put it on and walked outside into the Arab courtyard walking around pulling the hood up over my head and down over my eyes shading them from the sun feeling invisible. By now it was mid-afternoon.

I pulled the hood back and the Arabs were outside too prostating themselves on small mats jewellery glittering. There was another item of clothing with the great coat a jacket that didn't look so great but it seemed to have disappeared and I mentioned it to this disciple and he immediately went over to one of the others and tapped him on the shoulder, tapping him some more as the man continued his devout business ignoring him. Appalled, I walked quickly back to the house away from all this through into a corridor where clothes were hanging I rummaged through a few to find this jacket. There was steam everywhere. A *hamman*. Suddenly Bedaya appears, naked, in some confusion, as if lost. I am confused, vexed and anxious. What on earth is this all about.

"Somebody died today, I can feel it."

"Yes" I said, trying to ask questions, suddenly totally lost "*What is happening?*" But he gave me just a few quick words and bounded into the steamy *hamman*. He is still in action.

It is darker, Arab cops are appearing pushing people around muttering about dark practices in the steam.

I am frightened.

Bedaya said to me: "People are shit, my dear."

Typical of him, I thought. He didn't repeat the Old Man's dictum, "Some people are shit," he said "People are shit."

When Bedaya referred to man as The Bad Animal I didn't understand "*What is a good animal?*"

Now I do.

So Mr Green, for example, simply treats people as they are: Shit. He knows. He is shit and so are they. What is his game? To maintain false consciousness. To keep everybody right here where they belong. In the shit.

Bedaya gave me many warnings . . ."You have no idea what it is you're getting into."

But I knew pretty well what it was that I was getting *out* of

. . . And since I had no choice anyway . . .

I knew the call would come. 4 AM. A hoarse, whispering voice.

"I've seen Bedaya. I've *talked* to him . . ."

"Yes? Who is this?"

"You *know* who it is."

"I do?"

"Yes. I'm in Morocco. Somebody just tried to kill me . . ."

"They tried to kill you . . ."

"Yes" . . . a terrible crackling . . .

"Who is this?" The voice:

"You *know* who it is . . . very weak . . ."

A terrible machinegun crackling through the wires the voice still croaking . . ."The *horror* . . . the pain . . ."

"I can't hear you, there's an awful noise. How did this happen?"

"You hear me now?"

"Yes . . . what happened?"

"They tried to kill me."

"Who did?"

A terrible crackling crashing sound, the voice very weak . . .

"I can't hear you."

"You hear me now?" crackling through the wires . . .

"Yes, I hear that . . . and who is this?"

"*You* know . . ."

"No, the line is terrible. You're in Morocco?"

"Yes" . . . crackling, crashing . . .

"You hear me now?"

"Yes."

"It's J."

"Okay, J . . . What did Bedaya say to you?"

"He spoke about the Word . .. You hear me now?"

"Yes . . . And when was this?"

The voice, very weak, another sort of time . . .

"Two nights ago . . ."

"In the evening?"

"Yes."

"And then they tried to kill you?"

Crashing crackling

"Yes."

A long silence . . . crackling . . .

"You hear me now?"

"Yes."

"How do we escape from Time?"

"Uh . . . I suppose we can escape from Time anytime if we wish. It depends upon what you mean by Time . . . Bedaya is obviously in another sort of time . . ."

"But how do you handle it, the *horror,* the pain . . ."

Crashing, crackling . . .

"You hear me now?"

"Yes . . . I saw Bedaya at about the same time. He was naked, his body was whole again. He seemed rather lost and confused and that unnerved me. I tried to ask him questions but I couldn't pick up the answers. He gave me a few qick words and then dived away into a hamman. So he's still in action . . ."

"You hear me now?"

"Yes."

"How about Hassan i Sabbah's programme?"

"Well . . . I think it's still in operation . . . You know we intend to continue by means of the Third Mind . . ."

"Yes." The voice becoming clearer . . .

"I can hear you now." The hoarse crackling medium voice . . .

"Yes. Why is there so much opposition?"

"It's inevitable, isn't it . . . ?"

"So much opposition . . . To you . . ."

"Yes . . . ?"

"You know that?"

"I can imagine."

"I don't understand that."

"No . . . ?"

"Do you know where it comes from?"

"No . . ."

"You know the other J . . . ? You know who I mean?"

"Yes."

"You know he controls the Old Man . . . ?"

"Yes."

"You know who he works for?"

" . . ."

"You hear me now?"

"Yes."

"You know who he works for."

"I can imagine . . . The company, you mean?"

"Yes . .. You hear me now?"

"Yes."

"You have to be very careful. You know that."

"Yes."

"Do you think I'm crazy?"

"No. Is that what I'm supposed to think?"

"No."

"You just sound very weak and unnerved . . ."

"I intend to protect you."

"I think I need it."

"Yes. I want you to take this number. I'm going to give you this" . . . crashing, crackling . . ." number for you to call when it becomes necessary."

"Just a minute."

I dragged myself up and found a pen.

"Okay. Is this a London number?"

"Yes."

"And in what circumstances should I call it?"

"You'll know when Bedaya will tell you . . ."

"Okay, I've got it . . ."

"Okay . . ." Silence . . .

"Take care, J."

Silence a click and the phone went dead.

Mr Green telephones again . . .

"I have written an alternative version of your book   with a *surprise ending!*"

And some black-clad creep who says he is one of the ten men in the world who never sleep is on the job in Paris.

J phones.

"He won't sleep for awhile if I have to have a few words with him" he says.

He has his ways. KJ, colourful international fabulist . . . cocaine, champagne, whores, limmos, bodyguards, he really lays it on.

"Who is this character?"

"I don't know. It didn't happen to me."

"Yeah. I see."

"Says he's out of some kind of psychic institute on the Ile St Louis."

"Hah! I'll psyche him."

"Spends quite a lot of time out of his body, he says."

"Maybe he should stay out of it . . . They're trying to get at you through your vulnerable point, you know that."

"Yes. I know."

"And why is he so vulnerable to this sort of shit?"

I am lost for words.

My head is full of fog, like the mist that drifts over the river and trees swaying, at La Roche-Guyon . . . the water-like white stone village.

In the water like children . . .

Up up all the way up to the top of the rise . . . uphill all the way . . .

"*Well!*"

They reach the top and stare. They are both awestruck.

"I'd like to stay *here.*" . . .

"Yes, I know . . ."

He can't focus, he stares incredulously, luminous radiant into his eyes he falls on him holding his arms round his neck and trees swaying as the world spins . . .

Mr Green's "alternative version" arrives. Almost illegible in his shaking spidery hand, it is mercifully short.

In his version we both end up right back in the Princes Square Hotel to find that mad bitch — he calls her Freddie — waiting for us in the room. She is tidying up and keeping things in order she explains. I push her out saying we'll drop around and thank her sometime.

"Who's *we?*" she says. "There's only *one* of you."

The ashtray stops. On the very edge, people just get uglier.

"Okay" I say. But maybe he won't be so sure who I am . . . I'm not all that sure myself . . .

The phone rings in about ten minutes and whoever it is talking makes it very clear that he has known KJ much too well for much too long.

A real wrong number.

I have to take control of this goddamn situation Bedaya has left behind. No one else can do the job. Just typical of him to force my back to the wall.

My "allies" for the most part are devious, unreliable, or plain bone stupid. Sometimes all three. Bedaya's legacy.

The blackest, bleakest dawn. My head dropped back onto the pillow. I was in a car? — down Crow Green Road around into Orchard Lane horrified passing 68 twilight children playing in the garden "NO! NO!" — I was screaming — I have to take control of this I pushed my arms out ahead of me fingers forward and swept up flying along the street roof level the street getting longer and longer a wind turning me around I pointed toward a tree or large bush in a front garden to see if there was anything solid there but there was nothing an electric static as I brushed the leaves . . .

Well, Green Base. There where I would leave my body, early teens, staring at the chandelier, my head would drop. There was one period of weeks or months when I never went to school, the most mysterious . . . everything is hard to write about.

It has to be borne in mind that Bedaya's nerve was severely damaged by his illness in the early seventies. I wrote in the original draft of *'D' Train*: "He may have succumbed to spaces truly formidable."

He was vulnerable.

". . . This is bugged you think?"

"Yeah, doesn't matter just don't name names . . . As I understand it one of these psychos was originally wished onto Bedaya by Bavaria, right?"

"Yeah, as I understand it, a psycho-sexual attack. He's a born conspirator, as Bedaya once said."

"And what about the other little fucker?"

"Oh he was just one of a long line. He's a black hustler posing as a white boy. He came on very heavy right away. He was out to conquer . . . and didn't do so badly . . . neither of them did . . ."

"Yeah. Both crazy, one controlled, the other just a shark . . ."

"Yes, so anyway they were both seen on their way in due course . . ."

"Given the boot."

"Yes. The shark was given the boot by Bedaya in Paris then arrived in London and got the same reception from me . . . He was coming on like he had money   a *lot* of money   and we were all supposed to retire to the West Coast with him as manager   "

"Yeah yeah, he had his little hustle working. So they were both out, Bedaya reacted and you were on the ball, so what happened?   how did they get back?"

"The pressure in Paris was diverted to me   "

"Ah, I see . . ."

"This is where, we'll call her Freddie, comes in."

"Yeah, so they eased off rue St Martin and operations moved to St Lazare, is that the picture?"

"Exactly."

"What sort of creature is this one?"

"Oh, a medium, sob-sister type, trances, etc . . ."

"Okay, crazy, the same pattern. Any connections?"

"Yes, she's been controlled, to an extent . . ."

"Okay, I understand so he let her move in there and then she occupied the place, right?"

"Yes."

"So you weren't staying there anymore so you weren't coming to Paris anymore, right?"

"Yes. For quite awhile."

"In which time they had moved back into rue St Lazare?"

"Right. By the time I got back again Beday was very sick and they had control."

"Hmm. They diverted your attention. And rue St Lazare?"

"Well, she eventually came on with an evil eye routine engineered by some local clairvoyant she was getting desperate. It didn't work."

"She'd done her trick. By the time you got back Bedaya was being totally ripped off and she had almost totally fucked your situation also, right?"

"Right."

"*Financially* to the point that when you did come you were having to pay for hotels or I was and by that time they had Power of Attorney over Bedaya and were taking everything right?"

"Right."

The horror of passing through Orchard Lane seemed somehow false. I love these trips. It was idyllic there, sometimes. But by the time I was evicted hell had long since moved in. I've described all that. I would like to see the way they were then, the boys at school again. I would like a trip like that one night. The weather is variable, one day black and wet, the next bright sunshine. The temperature is moderate, even muggy. There have been terrible winds which turn the traveller around

"I went to the Princes Square Hotel today but it wasn't there . . ."

— ("the post office has been stolen") —

Twilight children

The light behind him has gone out. Or was it in front?

Merrymerry pipes   Louder and louder

An ancient phallic cult has re-emerged. They meet in dark flickering bars fading into toilets to worship the male principle . . . The cock is swelling thick at the base tapering off at the end into the other's mouth like a torpedo the world in flames around them. Teenagers stream into the cities like moths to the flame, burning. Panic-stricken agents of the Blue Virgin howl that God must no longer be referred to as He.

Too late. The phallic god is there at the end, here to go.

Closing time, Freddie

The music picks up. The current turned on.

A whiteskinned black hustler is served deportation papers in Paris.

Another retreats home to the family chateau, shattered, for his nineteenth nervous breakdown.

Higher and higher breaking the sound barrier whipping the Blue Virgin operatives into disarray.

Mr Green cuts out for the nearest airport the wind whipping at his coat tails.

"I'll get them *all*" snarls the vicious saint, drooling over his collection of wax dolls, stuck through with pins. "*All*. One and all . . ."

Well, you may get them *all*, saint, but what about the One?

Flashes of Blue Virgin operatives engaged in similar activities, muttering over their dolls

Burn your dolls, saint, burn with them, you'll like it, take your Blue Virgin with you for an immaculate consumption.

Glass explodes . . . "paean of victory and devastation . . ."

The Duchess of Wind is the Blue Virgin incarnate, patronising, condescending, manipulating, loveable, cheap . . . the naked grandmother playing for Time . . . those guys on Hell Walk they all scream: "*Dirt is her price!*"

As they parade their false tits and treacherous souls through the flares of ammonia, her agents every one . . . wax dolls.

Concerted psychic attack.

WE ARE VERY CLOSE

A smell that could take out an apartment. It smells like somebody died, or something — you can *smell* psychic attack — and that's the message: Die.

As the Old Man said:

"If you live through the fear, then you've got the courage, baby. If you don't" jackals are howling "you're dead."

Sitting at the table, me, the phone rang nearby, his questions about ten minutes today pointed toward a tree but it wasn't there today first or last tangle the wires the Old Man's voice then and you sat there, inaudible, aware that I was talking.

"As long as you have the strength to survive this initiation . . ."

I wake up at Susi's place calling for news of Bedaya. A muffled voice says there is none.

I got up and wandered around. She was preparing food and preparing to leave at the same time. The sunset was making beautiful reflections on a painting lying on the floor in front of the window.

"It was a good idea to put it there" she says smiling. She puts on her fur coat.

"So, no news" I say.

"Well, I have seen him, yesterday, he was very firm, haughty, not at all dissociated . . ."

We sat down on the floor in front of the door. She was talking about a spirit key . . . I must find it . . .

Services are affected. When I write only a summary gets through. A muffled voice. A fat bearded Greek greets me in a bar, as if remembering someone from another life. Bedaya stretched out on a large mattress surrounded by young people. He looked different, very quiet, preoccupied. The boys all turned to me as one group, shyly, but with authority and purpose, they know me, they've seen me before, in London I can't remember I was ill at ease, they urged me to stretch out over the mattress with them and our arms were around each other a thigh pressed up against mine I am nervous but fall back into a deep sleep.

Later, riding my bicycle very fast downhill along a country lane feeling good I stop abruptly at the entrance to a field and the boys appear, stepping forward to greet me, shy, impressive . . .

Back at the house I was preoccupied and anxious as usual, staring out of the window. That time, a twilight feeling. One of the boys whose name is Terry sat beside me and said quietly: "You have a problem with power . . . a desire for power . . ." I sighed, too weary to explain that I know I have been given power and I have to assume it somehow, no one else can . . . He smiles. "But this is the land of power. Everyone has power here ."

He urged me up, all of us were mounting an expedition to another house nearby, we climbed some steps to the entrance of this once grand villa and then squeezed in through a narrow window by the front door the red brick crumbling it looks as if a wall, or the roof, could collapse at any moment. Inside in a very cramped dusty room. People are expecting us . . .

It's difficult to know if this is happening now or if I am remembering something. Maybe both. Either way I remember so little. With the boys, we were based in the ancient ruins of a castle surrounded by a huge, otherworldly redbrick estate. We were being trained, rockclimbing on one occasion . . . a bearded man dressed in black with a fat strangely shaped body and very tiny feet gives us instruction . . . I seemed to be riding around on a bicycle or horse quite often, there was some glory at that time. A twilight feeling. We were all very close living under the threat of time slipping away. One boy and I were very close. I remember sitting with him high up on the battlements looking down his back against my chest head against my shoulder his hair on my cheek and it became terribly cold . . . And the battlements were full of tourists scrambling over the great rock we had once climbed and the light was going out and his head toppled over and rolled away over my chest as we both faded in time.

"That's a bit excessive" I thought — his head didn't have to drop off — and I tried to feel grief but I couldn't and it didn't matter anyway I was going too . . .

One centre, Moroccan, specialising in musical healing, is surrounded by a stereotype English village. I was assigned there as an assistant to learn something of the role of women in Time. I don't remember what I learned. I was out of the body and hovered around . . .

And we had to get to a bus station someplace, Juares, and I lined up for the ticket and Denis lined up with me talking and you sat there distracted, jacket open, tee shirt, distracted, and I bought the ticket and took the bus, Juares faded in time . . .

Stepping aboard, boats, buses, planes, trains . . . I was in time. Every day, all these people around me.

Bad weather has pushed up the annual inflation rate yet again
. . . the cost of living.

"The only great souvenir I have of my faraway past is a moment in the bus which led me to school every day no matter the day it was only the same with all these people around me I was trying to read the advertisements in the streets because I found I was too high in nowhere trying to be more real I wished in those moments that I could in the future meet someone who will belong to where I really come from someone with whom it won't be necessary to use words — someone who will know another language and who will be from elsewhere — because I was from elsewhere — because I was from elsewhere. Then elsewhere magically turned into a bed."

Trying trying to be more real I wished in my faraway past high in nowhere where I really come from.

Hexagram 12 rules the hour. Dazzling landscapes recede with the quarter moon.

Lost in the city . . . the bleakest street I have ever seen. Not a soul in sight, it receded into absolutely nothing, nowhere. Searching for the station . . . demonstrations flare up . . . A woman opens up a door in a wall and I go through.

Somewhere along the line we jumped off the train, a long long walk through the countryside, into the town and Bedaya was there waiting for me in the street with someone I don't know, we went inside, into a foyer and he somehow caught his arm in the elevator gate and tumbled over. He was back on his feet very easily with little help and we closed the gate. I suddenly realised who he was my head dropped onto his chest and then up into his eyes, firm, compassionate, azure . . .

"You don't want to cry" he said.

And always that time haunts us . . . that place where there was climbing . . . and where we knew who we were . . . locked in time our eyes searched each other . . .

The light is hurting my eyes . . .

"I pay for it . . ."

Fingers pointing to the sky   English time. Something dreadfully wrong with the weather.

What do you see as the benefits or objectives of the Third Mind?

Uh . .. well, "We want it to make a big difference, especially under the bed." (smiles) Immortal words of Ira Cohen . . .

I could collapse under certain circumstances. Like these.

So you were in Paris Christmas and New Year (1987) . . . ?

Yes, there was a sort of massed gathering, Friends of Bedaya, Inc. . . . And I was really given the treatment by experts in the business . . .

But I can accept that . . . the worst is always from those who don't even know what they're doing, and who feel bad about it afterwards . . . that's awful . . .

Why was someone like Bedaya surrounded by such awful people?

I don't know anybody who isn't surrounded by awful people . . .

Fear of being alone . . .

Do you see people as being totally corrupt?

More or less . . . corrupt, corruptible . . . it's inescapable to a great extent. There's a great potential for it. I don't think anything can be done without realization of that.

What can be done?

Well, do you embrace the corruption and join the ranks of the petty tyrants for life, as Castaneda says, or not . . . ?

So it all depends on the person really.

All depends on the person . . . And it's not wise to expect too much . . .

His face covered in darkness, left eye flickering . . .

"What did I do that was so awful . . . ?"

Do I know?

Young man writing . . .

"Continuity" — both alive

The writer is sat down on the bed and waits for the hero to wake up

it's becoming too late the morning is finishing — another empty day where there is no human feeling to tell nothing to write — "my book is my life my life is my book — "

Is it?

"You will open your eyes on a different land things are not the same. By the mouth you go into him and reach the centre — you heard the story of the Arabian cave where there are fruits and wine and tiger fur?

go into everything

"The writer is alone and tired, these sickly walks where there is nothing to see a dog pissing again an old lady goes back home no satisfaction to have there and no more here. What am I looking for?

" — Some air coming from the window. I take a great breath. There is something really happening now. Like a wave, it came inside me. I still can't believe in what we saw, I feel different when I close the eyes, now it's beginning to come over. I want to remember — "

Go into fruits and wine and everything   tiger fur?

The whole world is sleeping, sleeping, ponds freeze over the last long life, I feel different, dusty and dim, I want life's lost and lonely smell, alive on the bed, too late for the hero to wake up? There is no human to write . . .

What am I looking for? Everything. Some air. There is the window. The point is that we are trying to affect a change in every direction but it seems like we are only reaching the same place and I urge you to see what's really happening

What did I do that was so awful?

"Look, after a certain stage it wasn't a question of *if* you were going to be hit, but when. You were begging for it . . . And lemme tell *you*, if you think you've *really* been *hit*, you ain't seen nothing yet . . ."

Upstairs in the apartment Bedaya and I embrace and talk as the assistant hovers silently . . .

"It's been such a bad time" I said, hugging him tightly in reconciliation.

THE MAN FROM NOWHERE

When I first heard Bedaya's voice he sounded teasing, enticing, hard to handle . . ."Come around if you want" he said.

This was the man whose Intelligence background had taught him how to switch identity and rub out personal history to disappear into Morocco in the early fifties on the lam to re-emerge as Tangier restaurateur . . .

"Tall, broadshouldered, handsome with a cold imperious manner" he had left behind him how many different nationalities and identities? . . . painter, beachboy, writer, set designer, labour organizer, "phony 'von'," raconteur always, "*. . . superb, just the correct frequency of glacial geniality . . . Everyone will want to be the exception, the one he really likes . . .*"*

"The Man from Nowhere negotiated like a Tangier Space Draft on a Swiss Bank" nobody knew who he was anymore compiling a recipe book of magic in his spare time. A tricky business.

It was almost closing time for Magical Morocco. Electronic mind control was moving in and the Djnoun forces would soon be in full retreat gems to be snapped up before they disappeared forever. Spells and curses. Dance and trance. The Other Method was up for grabs. Tangier was the prognostic pulse of the world as the Old Man declared. Seedy operators packed the International Zone hawkeyed . . . The indefatigable Facility, Duchess of Wind (British Intelligence) trailing suitcases and native bearers across the Socco heading for the cheapest pension . . . She would keep a firm green eye on Bedaya for the rest of his life . . . the exception, the one he really likes . . . ? But he saw her coming . . .

"How long are you here for? And for any particular reason?" he said (she says).

They chased him out, eventually.

*William Burroughs, *Early Routines*

The old trick, waving so much money under your nose you really believe you're going to get your hands around a whole lot of it some day, soon — and then taking you to the cleaners. You'll never see another dime.

Green eyes on Bedaya for the rest of his life. Forever spells and curses. Time, a tricky business.

He was out with the shirt on his back, but a few tricks up his sleeve.

And in Paris of course the somewhat spectral figure of the Old Man rematerialized on the Place St Michel . . .

Scion of the same analytical faculty that led planets and eventually galaxies . . . post World War I days in the midwest, all those darkies singing sweet infancy, the brain, purgatorial, limitless and frightening potential vividly recreated . . . Graduated from Harvard in English lit. conceivably possessed of genius, studied anthropology, posed as reporter-copywriter-exterminator-bartender-private detective-only-living-American-novelist-cum-effective-adding-machine . . .

Faced with the prospect of terminal addiction in Tangier apartment flew off for several ultimately moving targets . . .

In Interzone they had kept a distance — Bedaya was averse to junk now, these two maverick agents, both born outsiders, were to join together to mount Operation Rewrite, an allout attack on the monopolization of Intelligence via the medium of Culture using as a model the eleventh-century Ismaili "hashishin" Hassan i Sabbah who terrorized Islam and beyond from his fortress of Alamut in northwest Iran — in this case from their old unnamed soon to be Beat hotel in the Latin Quarter. The Old Man was already in occupation. Bedaya moved in.

They were offering the Way *Out* — out of drug habit, out of identity habit, out of the human form itself.

"All anybody was ever supposed to want was to get back IN. Well, if you want to get IN instead of OUT then SPACE is not for you and you are going to get less and less of it until you don't have any at all . . . you've got nothing to lose but that worthless junk you're sitting on" Bedaya wrote fatefully. He provided the methods.

Bedaya's "life and sanity are at stake when he paints" the Old Man said. "He is exploring an actual place existing in outer space . . ."

In Islam the world is a vast emptiness like the Sahara. Events are written: *Mektoub*. Writing and painting are one. Bedaya's previously empty deserts became written deserts, written first from right to left like Arabic and then after turning the canvas from top to bottom like Japanese within a multidimensional cabalistic grid. Formulae spells to produce very specific effects in the viewer "This is latest way of revelation and way of action . . incredible discoveries in psychic exploration "

"Apply the painters' techniques to writing!" actual use of scissors on written texts years behind painting magical roots of art cut right through the pages of any book or images past present and future . . . lengthwise for example and shuffle scene from Marrakesh moving figures a street reminds you of a car phantom columns of text. Put them together at hazard bicycles cars read the newly constituted message. Do it. Take your own words or the words said yesterday or a boy on a bicycle years ago in fact the "very own words" of anyone living or dead everything you have experienced on the street. Put them in Islam. You'll soon see words and pictures. Cut through the word lines to see new flashes a second complementing the alpha voice off the page Japanese within a multidimensional cabalistic Interzone disappear across the Socco. The images past present future . . . *Mektoub*. Cut write through the writer. Events could be written and the brain produce an elaborate message hidden in any writing divined by dream images in brilliant colour an expanded ripple of meanings statements in moving figures cut right through the pages. Section one by section three section two by section four. Any combination. With any poem or prose. With *Him*. Try it.

Putting themselves together at hazard they merged into the third and superior mind disrupting the control lines via minds of others worldwide. ("The Old Man and I drew in the nets . . .")

Writing painting light shows permutated tapes stroboscopic machines. A big art.

"The Biological Film now showing on Earth can and must be rewritten!"

"Reverse the process, sexually and psychically Out into space "

"The means are at hand!"

"It was essentially an experiment which is still going on" Bedaya said, many years later. "An experiment which failed, but which is still going on."

By the early sixties the heat was closing in and their Beat Alamut was crumbling . . . and it was time to get the show on the road anyway . . . what else?

The years in London . . . The Old Man stayed there for so long because it proved to him that things actually were as bad as he said they were, Bedaya said . . .

It certainly is beyond me as to why anyone should choose to live in this dump, but then . . . Tangier was washed up, Paris anachronistic, as ever, and the US was still impossible for both of them at that time . . . London was cheap frozen and sedate and even seemed as if it might be on the upswing. Despite or rather because of its overwhelming awfulness cultural revolutions can happen in England like almost nowhere else . . . Cultural revolutions can be formulated in Paris — though not by the French of course — but that's as far as it goes . . . and you have to pay to live in that little piece of the past . . .

London in 1965 . . . and thereafter . . . was one of the deadest holes imaginable, even after three years in Adelaide, South Australia, and that's saying something. It was bleak, sinister. And this was on the upswing. . . . Things were happening there of course, but I certainly didn't see too much of it. By that time I wasn't looking too hard. I wrote my experience.

By the time I did "come around," to the apartment just off Piccadilly, things were very much into the downswing. Bedaya took my manuscript out of my hand and shut the door in my face.

The atmosphere in Dalmeny Court was heavy, oppressive, at least whenever I was around. Bedaya seemed rarely to be around. The Old Man was cantankerous verging on catatonic. He had worked, unfolding in his novels the soft step forward in human thought. Now it was terminal existence yet again . . . When the spirit's lost and the mighty fall . . . the land of the dead, yes . . .

I remember once somehow getting the impression that he'd cut his phrase "They do not always remember" out of my manuscript.

"Where did that come from?" I asked.

"They do not always remember" he replied, staring . . .

Their collaborators were just about wrecked.

Summer 1973, Antony, hagard, still young-looking, long black hair, bent over, clutching his stomach. He says Bedaya has told him to tie a string or cord tightly around his waist to protect himself.

"What is the thinking behind that?" he asks the Old Man.

"Bad spirits . . ."

Antony leaves. ("People are leaving us . . .")

And upstairs to Bedaya, resplendent, imposing, *radiating* a sort of intense dynamic gravity . . . The atmosphere is extremely strained . . . the Old Man moves around uneasily, Bedaya stands his ground in the middle of the room reading aloud from the *Herald Tribune* . . .

"'Hippies arrested and locked up at random'" he recites, rather loudly. "What kinda shit is this?"

"W-e-l-l . . . I don't think anyone's gonna take you for a *hippie* . . ."

We smoke a joint that doesn't seem to have any effect on any of us, they embrace and Bedaya goes down in the lift.

He was leaving for Alamut.

Up there, at over 10,000 feet above sea level, he experienced psychic attack as never before, so he said . . . total terror . . . He had always liked to be scared, addicted to terror "You've got nothing to lose but the worthless junk you're sitting on . . ."

Which is exactly what he did lose.

I didn't see him again until early '76, when, at the Old Man's suggestion, I visited him in Paris, where he'd returned "to die," or to further his career as a painter, depending on how he felt at the time. Ultimately of course it was not to be an either/or question. A stricken mage. It seemed difficult at the time to see how much longer he could last.

Bedaya was not a fearless man   he had diced and flirted with fear all his life, but now it had overwhelmed him. The man who wanted *Out*. Non-body experience. "For me, to know these spaces is to love them . . ." But what he had found there, finally, was sheer horror. From now on, everything was directed towards keeping the body, the ravaged physical body . . ." Some *other* kind of body, whether made out of some kind of incandescent metal or whatever   bull*shit*! What we're interested in is the body we have right now."

He lasted for another ten years by sheer willpower.

We warmed to each other immediately, as if meeting for the first time, and started to work together very quickly, we saw each other countless times and I become a sort of assistant-apprentice . . . the one he really likes . . . ? Well, that was the way he was. He was the greatest.

"If you can come in spite of these obstacles in Time and Space, use Jerry's telephone number until you have settled your ass in a whore's hotel in the quarter which will cost me about 20 francs a night . . . if your old hotel that you know can be had at that price, then take it and get over here for a pot of tea at twelve and slowly down to what laughingly we call work."

The things he let me see, made me see, I still can't see clearly . . .

These were the most exciting years, for me . . .

We set to work with tape . . . rue de l'Hotel de Ville, "setting down first the voice of one and, then, the voice of the other . . . ("as the dervishes desired.")

Unforgettable years of great pleasure and great pain; delight, psychic adventure and sickness unto death . . . such spaces he had guided me through.

I just find it so hard to remember . . .

Rue St Martin, him sitting at his table me nearby, both reading, my head jerked up and met his eyes, suddenly.

"What is it?" he said.

I gestured with my left hand to say — "Nothing. I don't know —" and my arm stopped, a perfect button hole had appeared on the inside of my sleeve and it was buttoned to my jacket. For a second I couldn't move. He sat staring. Bedaya's place where my head dropped just like it did in Orchard Lane and I was aware that I was talking to him, answering his questions, just before we met . . .

And later, when you were there, when he walked off into the other room and came back with an amazing tangle of wires attached to a tape recorder and holding onto the machine told you to untangle the wires and you sat there head swimming hopelessly pulling on these wires and I looked up and saw a blaze of colour around Bedaya lighting up the wall.

And before that, of course, he had guided me trancelike across the bridge and into the garden and given me his blue granules *lapis lazuli* on the tip of his forefinger . . . he was already beginning the process of leaving me behind . . . it would all depend on us.

He had guided me through to a new area of psychic, aesthetic bond

"You have to show him a higher level" is one of the few straight statements he made about the process. And he inscribed his spell on your copy of *Oeuvre Croisee*, once the property of Antony. He was extending the chain.

Parasites were moving in —

"The situation over here got ripe when Wolf ran off with Foutaise. Need I say more? When Foutaise dumped him, he went to Bill P. where he still may be for all I know. He is furious with me. Naturally. Bill tells me that he intends to write me anonymous letters! Ain't life strange. Since his whole swell purpose was to move me and all my works into his 'loving care' in SF, wasn't that an odd way to go about it?"

(Letter from Bedaya, 14 October 1982)

No, I don't think so.

For the moment he was too strong. But they would be back, eventually, with a vengeance.

How many betrayals of trust in this story? Between those named and those unnamed . . . By 1984 the operation was in full swing. You came to London and wrote:

Two candles are lighting the room creating a bridge to the other . . .

We were both waiting for it to be more strong we like that very much it's not too expensive for the price to pay even though you always pay it very much, honestly you could make it more precious if you like delicate spirit, wild as it can be . . .

Returning to the story we don't remember exactly what it was, knowing that it can be everything we decide to wait for it to be a little stronger And a thing suddenly happened suddenly the window broke and the wind enters the room destroying everything in its passage in five seconds the whole house explodes and crashes to the ground a virgin appears with all her stuff dressed in blue . . .

Now we are waiting for the candles to disappear trying to find what we have lost do we know when . . . ?

(Yes, I think we do . . .)

And you had already let it happen. "Something I knew was inevitable" I wrote later. But if only I could have stopped it. If only I could have seen what would happen . . . But Wolf and Foutaise seemed to have mooched out of the picture into oblivion . . . and I trusted you . . . If only I could have saved him.

But it was impossible. I was outmanoeuvred at every turn by predatory hustlers, Lithium-soaked terminal nuts, who had their orders of course. If there was something basically very *wrong* with a person, psychically, he was vulnerable, dynamically captivated.

"We confidently expect to see the Third Mind relegated to the archives . . . most profitably . . ."

Bulletin of Friends of Bedaya, Inc. ("Enemies are unnecessary") 1986 . . . An odious loosely-knit but effective team of wheeler-dealers and bloodsuckers, promoted by the CIA.

"Let's just keep this damn thing on the literary level, at least as far as the consumers are concerned . . ."

Through all his perverse and defensive about-faces and reversals of policy and management, forever washing his hands like the Roman emperor sick and disgusted welcoming the apocalypse, he stood by his dictum: We are here to go.

How could it be otherwise? It was obvious.

" . . . if you want to get IN instead of OUT then SPACE is not for you and you are going to get less and less of it until you don't have any at all . . . you've got nothing to lose . . ."

But now he felt he had everything to lose.

"So, one lifetime isn't enough, eh. Well, give me more! No! More!"

All that keeps us here is fear, he had said. And he was keeping himself here with fear.

I remember once, towards the end, rue St Martin, sitting around his table, he rather sheepishly and shyly said to the Old Man:

"Maybe to've opened ourselves up to all those dreadful spaces with all those drugs wasn't such a good idea . . ."

The Old Man talking quietly about various out-of-body experiences involving overdose, etc . . ." When it finally happens I expect to kick my habit in one concerted moment excruciating withdrawal . . ."

"But Bedaya" I said, "if it's so bad out there, well that's the place we have to go, so surely it's a good move to experience the area as much as possible . . . ?"

"Preparation, yes . . ." the Old Man said.

Bedaya looked down at the floor, saying nothing . . .

I tackled him, softly, about it later.

"What I meant is that it was a bad move to give ourselves the idea that such spaces actually existed" he said.

("So: there are no blue Little Hills and none of the rest is true, either. I condemn the whole thing . . .")

Fear of ultimately radical reality, fear of non-existence, trying to hold on and let go at the same time . . .

An insane mix of rhythm and melody, ranting voices car alarms police sirens dogfights and pneumatic drills.

The phone rang for about ten minutes today but it wasn't there, first the Old Man's voice then another, inaudible, a taped message. Whoever it is talking makes the ashtray stop "Bedaya wasn't playing games" I can hear a dubious assertion. And I couldn't move. Bedaya sat staring. Was nothing an electric static nothing — I don't know — sitting at his table me nearby, his questions, I pointed toward a tree or large tangle the wires and you sat there aware that I was talking to him, answering.

"What is it?" he said. His eyes suddenly lapis lazuli my head jerked up and met my body early teens staring — *"No! No!"* — I was screaming and swept up flying along longer and longer a wind turning into Orchard Lane horrified passing blaze of colour around Bedaya lighting up holding onto the machine he told you to untangle. My head the situation Bedaya has left behind . . . He walked off into the Other Room and left his legacy: *Sink or swim* . . . bone on the tip of his forefinger . . . heads swimming hopelessly they meet dark flickering back in Princes Square the world in flames around.

At the end, he was very calm. "After all, what is a heart attack? Does anybody really know?" I remember him saying.

Rhythm and melody ranting voices car alarms police sirens . . . trees spinning . . . world spins . . . they rise up up all the way up to the top and stare. Mist drifts over the river.

They scramble down to the white stone village.

You put a great emphasis on "Intelligence" . . .

The monopolization of intelligence . . . calling itself Intelligence . . . yes . . .

But are you really describing a conspiracy or just force of circumstance?

I don't know where you'd draw the line, really.

Well I was thinking, as with various cults, you know, they

Yes, they have to keep The Enemy, opposition, to keep them together . . . "Stimulated by opposition, we sought our position in time . . ." And people who may simply be suffering from neglect, indifference, like to see a great conspiracy, of course . . . it keeps them going . . . But as far as the Third Mind is concerned there has certainly been, and still is, great opposition . . .

Is anyone really "ex-Intelligence"?

Well, some types, perhaps refractory to control, are maybe left alone for awhile, if that's the way they can come up with something interesting . . . new directions, tactics, whatnot . . .

But then these directions and tactics might be published, available . . .

And they might not, but it doesn't matter, necessarily . . . everything is monitored, picked up by those who know how to use it.

Others will pick it up.

Well, if they don't know how to use it . . .

It sounds like a method of gathering chaos rather than intelligence.

Yes, well these are shortsighted, irresponsible adventurers . . . on both sides . . . reaping what they sow and trying to come out on top.

On both sides?

Sure.

You're rather ambivalent.

Well at the very least these Intelligence operatives have some idea of what they think they're doing . . . at least they're in some kind of control . . . then in contrast take these European cut-up artists, for instance, that's a joke . . .

Aren't you rather assuming the mantle of the Third Mind then?

I don't think it's something to be worn like a crown. The Third Mind is out there with the collaborators, as Bedaya said. It's for anyone concerned who can engage the principal in the right circumstances . . . of course the right circumstances are something of a rarity . . .

But how many people would want to engage?

Difficult to say, know, or care about, really . . . a person is either in that situation or he isn't . . . most people aren't, presumably . . . so the question doesn't arise . . .

Like an incubus. It could be you. Somebody with bones in the first place. As I sit here smoking in the mirror I drew in the net . . . you were expecting me. You've been here before . . . ? Human I twisted my mouth slightly. Sweet infancy, limitless and frightening, all they have to do is remember this insert. Faced with the prospect of what was forgotten or dissociated, us . . . The sun.

Dazzling early morning light on the water. I see fishermen drawing in nets . . . ?

Horror stories of rings pulled off Bedaya's fingers . . . Once Wolf went underground under dubious psychiatric care doubtless arranged by Friends of Bedaya, Inc., Foutaise went to the Marais apartment and cleaned it out, so the story goes. Wolf deported back to US. Very neat. Will Facility move in now?

There was a conspiracy to wipe out Bedaya and myself. I don't mean that I'm supposed to be such a great threat to those people but they'd certainly feel better if I went away someplace and never came back. (As you know, it's got so bad that sometimes I feel I'd feel better myself for that to happen.) Of course they intend to do everything they can to stop me getting any of that money.

But the whole thing is part of a bigger scene a big power battle, to neutralise and assimilate a lifetime of psychic power into three-dimensional financial manipulative areas and you know the amount of attention we received from those very powerful people they were feeling us up and down, trying to neutralise, assimilate, destruct . . .

I did practically nothing. I was stuck in London sulking because I couldn't come to rue St Lazare. Maybe I didn't have the money anyway, and I was getting books published, Bedaya's included.

Now that I think of it, at that time it was Facility who, typically, repeated what the Old Man said (she says): "He is sulking."

Well, I felt I had something to sulk about. And nobody would listen. Ah, that was a mess.

His judgement of me was very acute and censorious "sulking," "emotionally upset," when something was happening in Paris my response was just to stay away. Just as they knew I would. I played right into their hands. And I came back too late. Basically they had already taken everything.

I remember after you told me what had happened in rue St Lazare, I said to you: "I've lost everything." I think you may have understood that in a very narrow, egoistic way. You dismissed it with a laugh. The trouble is, when I said it, I was talking, thinking in a very narrow, egoistic way. I was hurt, jealous. So much thinking about my self and my hurt, that I didn't see I was really telling the truth.

But that "Don't insult my friends, the only ones who are really doing anything for me" attitude from you and Bedaya was really very hurting . . when I could *see* what was happening, and still didn't really believe myself — was I *simply* jealous? Everybody said so.

Impossible to describe that last night in Paris, that last night of defeat and retreat . . . living on your money, the roof caving in — we kissed twice at the gare

St Lazare — that smell that appeared saying *GET OUT! — GO! DIE!*

Experts in the business . . . waving so much money around under my nose I really felt like I was going to get my hands around a whole lot of it, some day — soon . . . taken to the cleaners . . . a few francs in my pockets . . . and the snow . . . and that train . . . we kissed twice before the nightmare — Snow snow and more snow and the Train pushing through — away — *out* — on and on to the frozen coast the end of the line a huddle of morose January travellers — twice before, the nightmare — three concerted appeals — snow snow and more and more snow the roof caving in on and on to retreat, living on that last night of retreat.

All the way back to nowhere, the English coast and a British rail ghost station and on and on and on crawling towards Shit City — once the train stopped for three hours —and more and more snow no heat nothing to eat or drink cops pushing their way through the corridor like they are about to put down some kind of uprising — this is England . . fifteen hours . . . Finally the train simply gave up and dragged itself back to where it came from or someplace I never want to see again . . . We never made Victoria . . .

18 Lancaster Road, "the flickering room, breathing, heaving" . . . dark, bleak, obviously finished, gone, no heat nothing . . . ensnared and disillusioned . . ."tired of yourself and all of your creations . . ." I sat shaking.

The expression of an intelligence that could *happen* defeated? by Intelligence . . . whores . . . ceramics classes . . . pasta . . . ?

I gave you a dangerous world to live in. Yes, I know it was already there, but it was me who handed it over to you.

Are things hopeless, has it already been done? I don't know how to answer. I don't feel that's true, but, for me, you know, I don't eat, I am strong, but it's very conscious, I don't have the money or the desire most of the time . . .

In London this time I found our walk through the park at night quite magical. But I felt a bit strange, suspicious at first when you started talking about the Star. I didn't know if you were acting, humouring me, and I felt that the star was something you'd put out of your mind, preferred not to think about. (There were times, since we saw it, when your attitude and behaviour made it seem to me that you had put it out of your mind entirely . . .)

(I've always felt very strange, confused about that star, just not knowing what to think . . . but it was an unmistakable sign, of course. How many signs do we need?)

I am here, still weak from not eating and not wanting to, last night in London very heavy, though I was okay . . . pubs almost completely empty, cops swarming around everywhere . . . They're building up a near-certain riot situation for the end of the month. I don't plan to be around, unless you are (ominous statement). You should see it. Quite a scene.

Vivid out of body experiences later in the night, being kind of pulled up by the legs, hovering over the room through the park at night quite magical. The night, pulled up by what happened in rue St Lazare . . . I was hurt, I think. How many signs do we need? Breathing all the way back to nowhere, I am here . . .

I'd like to emphasize this point about the Third Mind – Bedaya wasn't fooling around, talking about this marvellous thing forever. It was necessary to produce some actual physical product. Immediately we made contact he got right onto the job. In other words, words were necessary, but he controlled and chanelled them.

Given the facts as you explain them, isn't there a way of looking at it that once the "physical product" was achieved, it was perfectly reasonable for Bedaya to move on to another person?

Yes. But it's not as simple as that. The product can be extended, which it was, and that's where the opposition really came in –

The conspiracy . . .

The conspiracy just kind of fell together, into a concerted drive to take all that was seen to be useful out of Bedaya and dump the rest . . . so it wasn't so much a case of him moving on but of various parties moving in on him. They attacked him at his weakest point . . . and essentially the whole concept of the Third Mind was seen as unpredictable, unnecessary, and, most particularly, unprofitable . . .

Today the man from nowhere seems far away, remote, in a different time. I barely remember vital conversations . . . about collaboration . . .

"Yes, yes . . . will I remember all this later?"

"Perhaps."

He faded far away back into another sort of time leaving behind his delayed-action instructions.

This is a lot longer than a year ago . . .

Time is eight elbows and endless war, the ominous eighth month, threat of destruction, fall, fall, and rise again, remember vital conversations and rise again.

Streaks across the sky over La Roche-Guyon, far away.

"I don't want to let anybody down, living or dead . . ."

But will those alive, and longer than a year ago, dead, let me down?

Sometimes it gets so hard to see.

I have somehow neglected to record innumerable calls and encounters with Mr Green   charmingly, impeccably creepy. He really is off the set of *Casablanca*. How much of all this am I expected to explain?

I pick up the phone.

"*Lazare?*"

Yes, this is St Lazare in the ruins of a world, mask-faced, he who left everything behind him back in the world of men . . . wraps his frayed shroud around him, how creepy . . . his frayed world . . .

We will all die, perhaps without seeing somebody, ever again. But you never know. He may show up just to be there and guide you through that long long way we have all known and know so well . . .

The distant crumbling outside world. Ruined staircases of the chateau at La Roche where it all began . . . the conversion point . . .

So, we finally found our way there, not knowing we were going there, naturally.

And somewhere there, some Time, Bedaya left me behind, you too, well, he *pushed* you away, too much for you

On the steep slope of woodland alongside the chateau   dead of night   and directly he pushed your attention someplace you were lost

at least from my point of view, and maybe still are   presumably   then we were attacked   they were all in period costume . . . Stormtroopers maybe?

So we somehow finally found our way . . . Then the full force of opposition . . . Pushed you away . . . to someplace you were lost . . .   dead of night

"Lazare?"

The wanderers.

And somehow there, some Time, Bedaya still is   presumably   a world mask-faced, he who left . . . what a drag, those cold ears left me behind you too . . . not knowing we were going there, La Roche where it all began . . . the world . . . a world of men and women too . . . around him, how creepy . . . everything behind him back in the world was felt . . . . his frayed ruined staircases of the chateau, costumes, this was in the old days and directly he pushed your attention naturally.

Yes, this is St Lazare in the ruins of Guyon, far away.

Cold earth wanderers . . .
"You've been here before?"
I stirred my coffee listlessly.
"Appearances can be deceptive."
"That's what we're talking about,"
"Basically, I'm cold. I want to get *warm* . . ."
" . . . that's what you did, and you're seeing it . . ."
Interminably.

I moved to replace the receiver and saw it was already there, in place.

The Key, where will I ever find the Key?

— *Do you really think I don't know where you are?* —

So everything will be okay, as long as I have the strength to survive this initiation . . .

CHATEAU-ROUGE

In open country again you can breathe.
That is the theory, but our theories are untested.
Things are not the way they were.
How can we be sure? New laws apply;
and who knows the difference between the law and the wind?
And who knows the difference between you and me?

Lazare is not solid, posing on the trail of darkness . . .

"Having had your dream, *be* it . . ."

My head is full of fog, I see dim then increasingly vivid scenes . . . motorways, country skies, crumbling forts, city streets all around me . . . I walk through villages and strange resorts thinking of that poor creature in bed back in Lancaster Road, broke. I seem dim —

DANGER! — LIVE RAIL! — STAY IN YOUR CAR! —

And you turned — walking to your train —

Susi sitting on the floor, twisting and turning, writhing from the waist up like a serpent — she is demonstrating something —

An excruciating Belfast bawl from the front door

"*Whathefuckeryadoin?* — this myshtic shit — *Thersh people fuckin dyin out there!*"

Jesus Christ, KJ it is!

He reels into the room demolishing everything in his path trips over the cat and crashes onto the chaise-longue hauls himself to his feet again and staggers off into the kitchen to re-emerge ten minutes later howling:

"*I did it for Ireland!*"

He has eaten the dogfood.

After a few lines of coke, about half a dozen joints and some kind of aphrodisiac, he finally passes out.

I wake at what appears to be 1:30 PM, or 2:30. I pick up the phone to check. It is dead. I drag my self into the next room to try the phone there. It is dead. I can't focus. My face in the mirror is dim, blurred, fading away.

KJ has been up and about for some time judging by the trail of chaos. The cat is crouched shivering under the table in a condition of near dementia. The dog has apparently split.

The phone rang suddenly and I nearly fell over.

"'Allo — oui?" I croaked.

"Wha — ? — Some fuckin Frog — GEMME SUSI! — "

"It's *me*, Jim."

"Uh? — look you gotta get over here quick —"

"Uh? Where —"

"No — WAIT A MINUTE! — WAIT — Yeah, I'm comin there —"

"Jesus" I mumbled.

In the bedroom the windows are wide open wild winds whipping the curtains. Around the apartment I try several switches but the electricity seems to be cut. I walk through to the living room hit the switch and it lights up.

Somebody is lying on the floor. Maybe it's me. I have the feeling I should get out of here.

Susi comes back with the dog.

She had phoned me.

"James wants you to come."

A return ticket.

I phoned Bedaya. "You know about this?"

"Yeah, yeah."

Shortly after he phoned in total panic. One of the worst things I ever heard. George was there to advise him.

"*What are you trying to do?*"

"What? You knew about this ?"

It is winter and the people are scared to go out. The sun is shining through the trees like somebody's last dream. Time is an open and shut case a return ticket in solid eternity.

Bedaya saying, "I *have* to go."

Holding my arm.

I shall get used to it.

The *Ka* gets into three dimensional reality by means of a physical body. The body gets back via the medium of dreams. They are divided and need each other. Bedaya had been drawing me back into the area of my parallel body, now the only area in which he could be directly, consciously, contacted. The only way to reach him is to follow him there. An extremely perilous procedure.

In my other body I had heard him, seen him, touched him, heard him telling me: "*No more extra time*" . . . holding onto my arm . . ." I *have* to go." The Old Man was there also, both of them sweet, considerate, calm.

In my ordinary conscious state I had not remembered this at all. All I remembered was Bedaya voicing my own fear of entering into this other reality . . . "I'm so afraid." The Old Man: "Of course you are, my dear . . ."

Playing their parts.

At first, Bedaya was in a condition of amnesia. He felt that *someone* had died. He did not know who. Later, since there were no natural deaths, it occurred to him that he had been killed by a Madame Ba, but he did not know why. There was no time to think and it was also hard to see. For the moment it was one steamy hamman after another.

Bedaya rested.

Unless the development of consciousness is commensurate with the development of events you are in a mess. Situations are out of control. And your attempts to control only reinforce that situation.

The hamman has its advantages. Nobody is discussing how many times some body has gone to the toilet. Everybody is right there. Wherever that is.

So he rested, surrounded by his team, as ever. And he eventually pieced the story together.

He had been waylaid. That was a fact. In the present moment, he had to understand what to do about that.

Here, again apart from you, I have visions . . .

WE ARE FROM HOME

I looked up from my drink and found myself faced by two almost identical young men dressed in heavy black shoes, Levis, leather jackets, dark grey woollen shirts. They were apparently no more than twenty. The only way of telling them apart seemed to be by the slight differences in the cut of their jackets and their black hair. They were standing at the bar staring fixedly at me, just a few feet away. They had no drinks. I stared back, an odd numb feeling in the back of my neck. I knew they were part of Bedaya's team, although I couldn't remember them. They exuded an air of totally effortless superiority. I felt blank under the impact of their combined appeal.

They abruptly turned as if one and left, their movements slow and purposeful, almost synchronized. I was staring at the door. Wind seemed to be ruffling my hair as if they had left it open and then I was confronted by something truly awesome an angry-looking blood-red planet a burning world spinning in space advancing closer and closer and I heard a voice I knew to be that of the two boys:

"*We are from Home.*"

And I was back in the bar. I rose unsteadily and left.

I awoke with a start at about 5 AM. I was in bed. I don't remember how I got there. All I remember is approaching them in the street and then them abruptly pushing me into a narrow alley and somehow pummelling my body with the flats of their hands, chest, back, thighs, stomach, I didn't feel at all alarmed I simply felt weak, totally unreal, and their concerted blows pummelling the breath out of me. Everything went black.

I sat up in the bed, staring into the blackness. Had it been a dream? . . . or had they taken me Home?

Night and its shades commune . . . I am being squeezed out of the world. I don't know how much longer I can hold on, or why. There are battles of the night. How much longer I — ?

So he had been through all that and then something, someone, had stopped him. Concerted blows. What? Who? Everything went black. Staring into the blackness. Had it been a dream?

Frustration and obscurity. The sky is behind me. I remember little or nothing.

He remembered that his old friend and adversary Madame Ba had insinuated her zombie relative into his life. Foutaise, who was back out of the nuthouse and installed in an apartment with his "girlfriend" Freddie, a "fatassed terrorist dwarf" as Bedaya called her, a poodle, Fifi, and his collection of muscelemen mags. All girls together. Given his orders, he used every manoeuvre and manipulation known to woman.

Bedaya was literally possessed. It felt like a virus, he said. His journal entries for the period are painful to read. He had wanted — needed — to give Foutaise everything, and Foutaise was there to take it — *everything*. Basically oblivious to any of Bedaya's knowledge, the price he — She — demanded was capitulation, Bedaya's total ruin.

Madame Ba's strategy. Bedaya would love his enemy. As she did.

A dark shadow hovered over him as he slept.

Because existence as I have known it is slipping away, I do not flap about like a beached fish. I live in an increasingly black world, split in two. I am staggered by the mirror — as the blackness approaches — the eyes helpless and aghast. Two lone figures in a deserted street as the sun goes down, blood-red. A dream I'm living to the end.

Later I woke suddenly and fearfully. It was a fear connected with the two boys who I somehow knew spoke in tongues. They were threatening in some way. Then I was walking along the rue de Dunkerque — when? — looking for a bookshop that would have material on such child prodigies and I saw them across the street. I stared. They were *very* young then, seemingly no more than fourteen or fifteen, standing on the street with a third man dressed in black as if they had just materialized there. It seemed as if they were about to put on some kind of performance, like a freakshow. I found it offensive that the man should use them in that way. I walked on, dissociated, in another time.

Scenery shifted and then some way, some time, I don't remember, I visited them, they had a small office in Les Halles. There they were, seated at two desks, dark suits, white shirts, ties, reserved, friendly. I can't remember the conversation. It was confusing. There was some sort of tax official there also and one of the boys was taking care of him while the other who seemed somehow younger and more vulnerable received me with a slightly uneasy cordiality. It seemed to me as if we all at least he and I had the same problem. We couldn't quite remember. His eyes kept drifting uneasily to the area of my jacket pocket. I smiled. I was carrying, very strangely, a small sharp knife I use for opening envelopes. I reached into my pocket and pulled it out. He stared at it.

The meeting ended abruptly.

"How old are you?" I asked . . ." You could be any age."

He seemed totally lost, his head jerked around to the other boy who was bringing his consultation with the official to a close. For a moment it seemed as if he was going to babble incoherently in an alien tongue. His face contorted, his mouth was open and he was gasping.

The official was leaving, oblivious to all this.

"I'm sorry" I said to the boy. "Did I offend you?"

He didn't reply. He was staring at the other boy.

I repeated the question but there was still no reply.

I rose smiling. The other boy nervously asked if I thought his interview with the tax official might be useful. I said I thought so. Their discomfort amused me. It made a change.

"Excuse me" I said, still smiling. They smiled back uneasily. We shook hands and I left.

The encounters with the two boys crush me. Basically implicit in their attitude is their authority and disdain. And I know why. Or at least I think I do. I do.

Like Bedaya, I never thought this could happen to me. But who could really have ever done it to him but himself myself?

Bedaya was moving steadily through the Bardo, which he had described, in great strength and weakness, years before. He knew all this, he knew everything.

To continue existence you have to *pay* . . . and the price . . .

The person I no longer was had died with Bedaya. I now knew that. For a short while, after the experience at the white-stone French village of La Roche it had seemed as if I could still remain that person, and I had hung on for well over a year, in a condition of near-total pain. It was now no longer possible.

In time, the boys showed up again at the bar I frequented not far from where I lived in Notting Hill. They sat for awhile looking around and then I suggested we go back to my apartment to talk.

Immediately we were inside I started rolling a joint. They stared impassively. I wanted to see if they would smoke.

"We can smoke some if you want" said the older boy, as if it didn't matter one way or the other.

They walked around the apartment slowly, staring intently at Bedaya's paintings. They paid particular attention to a calligraphic message headed The Third Mind, addressed to me from Bedaya, January 1979.

The older boy turned to me and accepted the joint.

"You know, Bedaya was a master at casting pearls before swine" he observed cuttingly but somehow completely without rancour.

"He became the weak centre of a weak circle."

The younger boy looked up. "The problem was his relationship with all those poisonous women" he stated flatly. "That awful so-called Duchess, Windhover . . . Madame Ba and all her puppets . . ."

"You know Foutaise and Wolf were a team" I said.

"Yes. Why wasn't something done about that?" he snapped, with some disdain.

"Yes, why wasn't it?" I retorted.

The older boy handed him the joint and turned to me.

"We were in no condition to do anything about it . . ."

Again I caught his implication. I was rolling another joint.

"It was complicated" I said.

"You know, of course, that another person appeared in your life at the same time Foutaise attached himself to Bedaya — didn't you see that this was the beginning of an offensive against both of you?"

"Against us *all*! And they both fell for it — *completely!*" the younger boy almost yelled.

"I was working on my own" I snapped back. "Completely alone. Where the hell were you when I needed advice?"

"We were not even here — here on this level" the older boy replied calmly.

I stared at them.

"I see."

I stood up and walked around a little.

"Why are you here now?" I asked.

"To see what we can do . . ."

"Hmm . . ."

"With your situation you'll remember that you were once forced to smash the glass front door of an apartment block in Paris . . . ? We've seen that . . ."

"Yes, rue de l'Assomption" I mumbled. "I've written about that . . ."

"That should have been the breakthrough, or the breakdown, but it wasn't . . ."

"No . . ."

"And you let things drag on and on until he finally let this controlled agent, this woman, into his apartment to live and he's still so ignorant —"

"'Ignorant' shit! — he's controlled" the other boy interrupted.

"— and arrogant that he can't even see that she was controlled — and you let all this drag on and on even though Bedaya frequently urged you to stop it because it was becoming so dangerous . . ."

"Apart from anything else" I said wearily, "I had had no other place to stay in Paris. Bedaya could have done something about that . . ."

"He was too weak!" the younger boy finally exploded. "*Because he had been outmanipulated and outmanoeuvred by a bunch of shitty neurotic poisonous ventriloquists' dummies! — a bunch of women of both sexes!*"

The other boy gave him a sharp glance and he calmed himself.

"I know, I know" I said quietly. "But you know and I know that he was basically outmanipulated and outmanoeuvred by himself . . . nobody could do it better . . ."

My voice trailed away and we all three fell silent, saddened.

I looked up from the floor.

"Why were you both so intent on the Third Mind calligraphy?" I asked.

They both stared back, saying nothing.

After awhile the younger boy spoke, now calmly and quietly.

"We don't remember anything. We remember what should have been the first time seeing you, on the street in Paris, but it wasn't . . . Bedaya had put us there on that street, he was there, and he was making us move in some way, make these gestures, I don't know why . . ."

"I think it was just to attract attention" the other boy interjected.

"Something. I don't know. But it seems like before that we met you with Bedaya in a school of some sort, I could remember but it's so hard, here there were others there also and even then we seemed to remember you in London . . ." He smiled. "And in Les Halles, which seems much more recent, but probably isn't . . . Time is such a problem . . ."

I smiled back.

The older boy seemed deeply moved.

"The school was the scene of one of the first great defeats" he said. "I remember that. We had to regroup after that."

"That's what we have to do now, isn't it?" I said.

They stared back.

"We are not kids, you know" the younger boy said.

So we were in some kind of training establishment at some time or another . . .

Staring deeply into an abyss of Time. The old cycle was about to close. They would be overcome. Bedaya had known many such defeats and retreats, but for some of the others it would be traumatic. To put it mildly.

"What would you say are the main events in your life, as you remember it?" the older boy was asking.

"Well" I said, "Australia and all that, and arriving back here ... when I was about your age . . ." I smiled at the younger boy. "And then meeting Bedaya, and the Old Man . . ."

"And then Vogue . . ."

"Yes, yes, and then Vogue . . ."

"He was the first member of our team that you really contacted, here."

"He is not a real member of our team because he doesn't know what he's doing" the younger boy interjected.

"That's not true. He does know, as much as any of us do "

"Wait" I said, "You know I've always been on this level where it seemed like he was someone who had to be indoctrinated, inserted into the team . . ."

"No. Why would you have had such a feeling for him if he were not already a member of the team . . . ?"

"But those are all memories . . ." I said. "Remembered in a framework of ordinary human time . . . There are other memories, which don't fit into that framework . . . of another time . . ."

"Yes, we remember being in Bedaya's school . . ." the younger boy mumbled as if to himself.

"Is it possible to define exactly what we were being taught there?" I asked.

"Yes, it is" the older boy replied. "But it's so difficult to remember everything, or anything, here, nobody can . . . but we're much closer to it than you. Bedaya was using the Other Method to teach a 'true and different knowledge', obviously. He had trapped a few souls and was getting on with the job . . ." He paused, a little lost. "That's as much as I can see. Maybe we'll get closer to it later . . ."

"Vogue was there, being taught there?"

"You were there sometimes when he was there . . . He is from another cycle . . ."

The younger boy laughed unexpectedly. He was smoking the joint.

"I remember him, he was funny . . . a strange, chaotic guy . . . When we saw that you and he had to team up it was such a laugh! . . . What a team! a comedy act!"

He started laughing uproariously as we both stared at him a little lost for words.

"God, he's too much!" the older boy mumbled.

Suddenly I couldn't control and broke into laughter also.

"We *must* remember everything we can" the older boy was saying imperatively. "Otherwise we're lost and *alone here . . .*"

The other boy fell across the bed laughing hysterically.

I AM NOT ALONE

(Chateau-Rouge)

And so, like Bedaya, we eventually pieced it together.

Into an abyss of Time . . . amnesia, out of control . . . about 5 AM. I was in bed, staring at the door. All I remember is my hair. My head dropped "a bit excessive" everything, something, someone went black. Staring into the blackness, Madame Ba's strategy: blood-red . . . Walking along the rue de l'Offensif, material in another time . . . kept drifting uneasily . . . Basically implicit staring at the other boy, still no reply. I know why. Or at least I rose smiling "But who could really have total pain?" the person I no longer was looking around an apartment block in Paris Bedaya: "You must remember this place" On the street in Paris Bedaya in London, and in Les Halles which street? He was there. There were others there also they stared back in great strength together. And great weakness, years. He knew all this, staring deeply he knew everything, anything, memories.

Bedaya and somebody who had to be the Old Man. Others, using the Other Method of another Time.

The centre was just one in a series of strategic locations. But for us it was *the* centre. The Chateau . . .

The laughter was the key. The time spent at the chateau had been one of delight, excitement and, quite often, hysteria. I have a feeling that the two boys remember more than they say, but they are not telling me. I don't blame them. But Bedaya had obviously kept them on another level of extremely heightened awareness since birth. They had little or no contact with ordinary human time. Bedaya's laughter . . . "You feel you've lost your youth?" he asked once. "You're right! You have!" Choking with laughter . . . genuine delight . . .

We have never known any moment that was not part of our training.

It is difficult to define what, or how, we were taught there. We were just there. A lot of the training was practical, physical, rock climbing is the one I remember the most, and I think was designed to teach us how to live and function on that level. We knew our goal to be freedom, of course, but since there we were free, seemingly, it was rarely ever verbalized. And we were always, increasingly, aware of a hostile, encroaching force, determined to destroy us.

And, behind it all, always Bedaya's voice . . . teaching an alternative version of history and manipulation of power.

Free or not, we were continually very high. We remember how it was there, of course, high up in an eternal midsummer there we were . . . over the trees and the river, a veil of mist . . . when we finally found our way back it was all there waiting for us, just like that . . . ecstatic . . .

"You said that Vogue and I had to team up" I said to the younger boy. "Why was that?"

"Too neurotic" he mumbled as if disinterested in the subject.

"He was strangely blocked off, shut away" the other boy said slowly. "He must have been traumatized at some time in some way. He needed a one-to-one contact . . . Bedaya set up your first meeting here, of course . . . He set everything up, he couldn't stop setting things up. Eventually he set himself up . . ."

"He was always full of such tricks!" The young boy was laughing again. "I remember when he brought me to his place once while you were there and told me I had to act like a chicken in front of you, clucking around the room. I did and he made you see a real chicken, right there in front of you . . . ! — you were — " He couldn't continue, almost collapsing with laughter.

"To shift your consciousness a little" the older boy said. "Do you remember . . . ?"

I nodded . . .

— Momentary blackout — the room swirling around and around

lying back head supported by his knee as he flickered his fingers in front of my eyes repeating a word out loud in front of me a name whose name?

"I found I was too high in nowhere trying to be more real I wished in those moments that I could in the future meet someone who will belong to where I really come from someone with whom it won't be necessary to use words someone who will know another language and who will be from elsewhere because I was from elsewhere . . ."

("*God! You're so difficult!*"

"I know! and *you know* that I'm trying to do everything I can to handle this situation under *such pressure*! What more do you think I could do?"

I was suddenly and inexplicably very angry. I felt as if I might explode.

"I don't know . . .")

"Dear brother, don't cry!" the young boy was suddenly kissing me

"*Stop acting!*" I snapped.

He started back.

"Yes, he's a little crazy, the same as all of us in this situation . . ."

"Shall I tell you the real reason you and he had such difficulty . . . ? You needed something like the size of a chateau, to be together . . ."

The young boy was clapping his hands furiously. He suddenly had a joint to his lips threw it down it hit the floor and shot back into his mouth.

"A good trick" I said, my head swimming furiously

"*Let go! Let go!* Remember the Chateau to be together! "

You will be slaves in a castle . . .

I looked up. He was reading aloud from a poem by Paul Bowles . . .

For every bottle there will be a pupil.
We are free and can climb mountains,
But for every passport there is an entrance . . .
Grains of former mosaics haunted us
And for every shred there was a sob
And for every stab there was a silence.
For all our freedom we had been chained,
But for every laugh there had been a caress!
But for every love there had been a smile.

The young boy was clapping his hands — *smile*. In a bar, my contact has not arrived. Your shoes hurt my feet — *sob*. Chateau to be together! — Delirium. Bedaya had set us up. For every passport there is an entrance and he had so much difficulty. Set up by Bedaya as a warring couple, which after all seems to be the role most fitted to us, for protection. Appearances can be deceptive. Everybody there was playing some part or other, usually in pairs. To keep out the daytrippers . . . even then crawling up towards us in their caravans . . . All other human beings are a threat . . . forces of Madame Ba, who no doubt was watching it all in a crystal ball in her imperial toilet, down over her golden bowl, haunting us . . . for every drop there is a deluge . . . And for every deluge? The Word can fall down like this. And for every shred there is a life. Journeys. Delirium —

"Let's go! Let's go!" — Remember there we are free and can climb mountains! Shall I tell you the real reason human beings are a threat . . ."

There they injected us with a drug they called: I am not alone. All in himself dark on the red material I see him pass and then together following the middle line cutting the image that takes us naked. Vomit and dust will come to dress you I'm losing my time I'm not alone let me bring you I don't know during orgasm I'm going back with him the light the youth your shreds your silhouette I vomited and ejaculated our bodies to join him several times and consume myself. I forget. Falling tapes of hungry laughs. Cruel simultaneous ejaculation. I am the senses and I am twisting.

A metallic whine and the covers are being sucked off the bed and I am swept up into the familiar grey room last words gurgling in my throat.

A small room, made of glass.

"The effect of that drug we were given lasts a very lot longer than it appears to . . . It starts in an area of sheer delight and then goes slowly and steadily through to where the two egos are totally revealed . . . usually a most unpleasant spectacle . . . and beyond, to where the egos are vomited and ejaculated . . . The whole history . . . of the history of the Word, is the history of the ego. A deadly trap. We are here to break this . . . to *cut* the image . . .

"He has now been almost totally taken over by his cover story, as was expected. He is fighting himself and all these things. Conflict is his element . . .

"You needed to fight, for *strength* . . . Bedaya set you up to give you strength. There was a concerted attempt to either kill you or drive you crazy. If you survived . . . It was sink or swim . . ."

Swimming furiously   in chains?

"And I still love him . . . Isn't that incredible . . ."

DISPLACED PERSONS

In a car with Mr Green looking for La Roche-Guyon. We come across a sign pointing to some delightful spot he and I remember very well and we want to go there. When we arrive, to nobody's great surprise, the whole place is totally wrecked. An area of shady trees alongside the river has gone down under the bulldozer. I ask the driver if he knows how to get to La Roche from here. He says yes but some way or other we wind up in the main square of a big market town. I walk around a little and then back to the hotel where Murray is waiting upstairs to introduce me to a group of gentlemen practitioners of the Great Game . . . Oldfield & Co. . . . Kincora, all dressed in Edwardian style, smoking . . .

I decide I have to make it to La Roche alone, I try a train and a bus but time defeats me —

A voice from the past saying: "The Old Man is going to follow Bedaya." Bedaya was leaving, finally. A, to me, suspect member of our team kissed him on the cheek but I turned away. We were supposed to have kissed him simultaneously. I felt embarrassed but I said "I don't care for such demonstrations." "Yes" said Bedaya, "that's just oppressive." I accompanied him outside and entered the bus with him   the Old Man was there

"Well, a little demonstration" I said, smiling and we kissed. I got off the bus and broke down

Suddenly in rue St Lazare I realised what had happened

So we penetrated the laughter and delight through into an area where it's how much can you really take of somebody else's soul?

The second time we were given that drug, as we moved closer and closer I was right through into an area where I was afraid of your eyes.

They were threatening in some way. But I couldn't confront the fear. *He who does not confront is attacked.* Well, he who does is attacked also, quite often.

Tea with Mr Green (who has now changed his name to Limpwell) chez the Duchess (she signs her cheques with the family name, Windhover, making a remarkable meal, somehow, out of FACILITY WINDHOVER . . . She is not a real duchess you understand   the pain of her life   but what they call a Natural. Quite bright . . .) We gritted our teeth, heads reeling under the interminable litany of her property speculations and manipulations . . .

"I've had a *particularly* busy day today" she blasts. A voice like a police siren.

"Ohhhh?" Murray drones wearily.

"Yes. I've been to see a flat in Mornington Crescent. *That* is if you've ever *heard* of Mornington Crescent."

"Oh, yes. Yes, yes! Yes, indeed."

"I nearly took it. £78,000."

"WHAT?"

"It was so beautifully converted. It really had everything. Dreadfully small of course. And poor view. The back was poor. Looked into a —"

"But what a terrible price!'

"You know, Murray, you really must be out of touch with reality. It was *small*, yes. But it had atmosphere and Mornington Crescent   a place you've never heard of   is going up in value like a rocket. Tomorrow . . . it doesn't . . ."   I found I was beginning to lose words, an almost imperceptible white mist   " . . . well, no, it is, perhaps a bit steep. But in a few weeks time it'll be worth *much more.*"

"I know" Murray sighs.

The resident sycophant shows up (an ageing bit of a number who restores antique furniture) takes one look at the mercifully meagre pile of dried up cakes and mouldy brown bread   (*"It's only penicillin!"*) and shrieks:

"FACILITY! How *divine*!"

Then my head really spinning and I don't remember   Facility asking about "your work?" Me replying "I'm halfway through a book on croissants. It's a love story"   any information given to Facility will eventually be used to your disservice — Murray seemed to have gone and then he was back again — a voice saying "I finally had what I always wanted. Lying on my back with his head on my chest. His legs were in the kitchen" . . . and then everybody seemed to have gone.

I don't know how I got out of there or what happened. I was in a car. Another car alongside of me and Madame Ba's ageless face twisted with hate and grief snarling curses and imprecations at me, as if she'd just emerged from the family mausoleum. When I made it back home there were cuts bruises and abrasions down one side of my body. Like teeth marks.

I discussed the matter with the two boys, as by now was the custom.

"Well, at least we didn't leave you with any cuts or lacerations . . ."

"Not physical."

"Bedaya told us we had to do that to you, the first time we met again, here."

"Yeah, and Vogue was set up to attack me, and Madame Ba and Windhover . . . I think maybe I need to hire a bodyguard . .. it's getting kind of *painful . . .*"

The young boy was giving me a strange, unnerving stare. "Of course, if you had someone with whom you could discuss this, in a situation of real solidarity, it wouldn't be so painful . . . would it?"

"I'm discussing this situation with *you*!" I exploded. *"And I would like to know exactly what the fuck is going on here!"*

The older boy was looking down at the floor uneasily.

He looked up.

"Look — you have a few bruises on your arms and legs — I hope your hip isn't chipped — but some people are *dead* . . . Please tell us exactly what you remember . . .

"Uh. Well there's not much more. It . . . felt really like going back in time, going back to try to forestall Madame Ba's offensive . . . I went back further and further — my mother was there, it was the 1950s and it was great . . . I told her how great it was to be there . . .

"Then there was the car. Madame Ba was young . . . it seemed possible to appeal to her. I tried to. We spoke but a bodyguard of her's showed up — I said: *'Take off!'* — and then there was some kind of attack and I don't remember . . ."

They stared intently, as if in awe.

"She could have killed you . . ."

"Uh. My mother, you mean . . ."

The atmosphere was extremely strained and they left. I wasn't sure if they were in awe of my daring or of my stupidity. Either way, I was too tired to care.

What is the general theme of this book?

Well, it's wider in scope than *'D' Train,* which really just focused on the relationships between the two minds. This one deals with the general situation within which all this was happening, and brings into focus other characters not previously mentioned . . . particular attention to events as they transpired after Bedaya's death . . .

There's a scenario you're presenting though, of a kind of ancient psychic tradition . . . ?

Yes, an ancient tradition and system of training.

Presided over by Bedaya?

Yes. There's the situation there where by the time Bedaya left us he had set us up into an area of total conflict, myself and the others involved. We found ourselves in a situation of conflict not only with the natural enemies of long standing but also with other members of the team . . . all of us being driven a little nuts by the whole desperate mess . . . in one case, for example, forgetting his cover story . . . forgetting it *was* a cover, and acting in an almost totally destructive manner. And I particularly found myself subjected to the full force of all this.

Why did Bedaya want to set up such a situation?

To give us strength.

But as I see it, didn't Bedaya reach a point where he was urging you to put a stop to your side of things because it was becoming such a danger?

It was more of a suggestion than an urging at the time. But yes, he did . . . I didn't. And we were both totally outmanipulated. It killed him.

Did you feel bitter about that?

Of course.

You wrote that Bedaya said people are shit.

Yes, this is the realisation that there is something basically awful in human consciousness. It came from his knowledge regarding secret documents which passed through his hands during his wartime translation work for the US. That was all the proof he needed. He managed to live with that realisation and to come to terms with it. His power in fact came from living with and in the area of special knowledge . . . There are those, like Bedaya, actively opposed to this basic situation and there are those dedicated to propagating it.

Isn't it essentially the ego which is dedicated to propagating it?

Exactly.

A firm grip on my arm I turned and there was one of the boys. I couldn't see which.

"Ah" I said.

"You know where we are?"

"Yes, yes . . . we arranged . . ."

"Walk" he said in a muffled voice.

I tottered along as best I could with him still holding my arm, pulling me along. It felt like trying to walk on a mattress, afraid I might fall off the edge of the earth.

"Ah. Take a look at this one"   his voice.

I stared.

Homing in and hovering in front of me was some kind of sickening shimmering horribly malevolent energy mass undersea tentacles whipping out of an old deeply corrupt core in all directions, flopping and bobbing around like a drunk trying to pull an imaginary dog on a lead. I stared, appalled.

It receded very abruptly and disappeared.

"*That* was an *enemy*!" I said.

"Just an average unpleasant human being" he laughed. "No, he was a bit much. Totally occupied. Some people are little more than that awfulness."

He stopped. "You realise we're just walking in the street, looking around . . . ?" he checked.

"Yes, yes."

"But that is the area hidden and maintained by the ego in each of us."

"Where did it disappear to so fast?"

"He retreated underground" the boy smiled.

His name is Terry.

We had all known horror, of course, before taking the drug, but, before that, we were really quite innocent . . .

"If you don't face up to what has happened you will be obsessed and oppressed by it for the rest of your life . . . I was *not* wrong to say there is so little time. If you think there is endless time you are going to waste it until there is no time left to waste . . ."

And his voice faded, sun caressing my face until the figure disappeared by an arch of roses down on the stone.

"Couldn't you both come around to meet these spirit guides?"

One of them stood motionless up against a crumbling brick wall face blurred, fuzzy, a spirit form I am conjuring . . .

Shielded my bare knees, early morning and I am in the garden, only in a blanket wrapped around me my mind felt suddenly very clear and

"You hear me now???" legs, the soft hair of the thighs (it was you) spilling the colour of roses we are something absolutely *terrible*! I saw Bedaya sitting at his table . . . the unmistakable voice . . . the sun and french windows of the chateau stone garden of an empty canvas . . .

"All the fault of those fucking contractors."

Through the windows the trees are shimmering, dazzling. I stretch out my arms and fly forward

"*Look*, listen carefully. We're going to walk from here to the restaurant . . . Time for the whole affair to be reviewed . . . the non-dominant brain area, you won't remember much until later . . . blurred and fuzzy flashes of taxis and street markets it'll just be an average lunch with the Duchess, maybe a bit subdued . . ."

"I'll remember you saying that . . ."

"Maybe. If you read it . .. The difficulty will always be to remember ."

And I remember . . . flashes of taxis, street markets . . . I was flying . . .

flooded is my name through you (I remember you saying that) blurred fuzzy taxis fly forward — *I am in the Ka* — consciousness penetrating right through the ego — Just an average memory, going to walk to this restaurant with the *Ka* — The Unmistakable Voice — Look listen carefully — We are shimmering, dazzling — I stretch out — consciousness flying —

Through the door. They see down into unconsciousness. We sat and talked. Again. Night. The police are at the door. *Ca va, ca va*, I mumbled, dazed. I cower at the corner of the window. Man staring at me with genuine concern. Me in the dark. My head had dropped to my knees. Sweet head, feeling the infinite desire was almost beyond caring. A strange graffiti-scratched staircase once ornate and I knew you, I said. He looked concerned. The great noise from outside. Wind whipping into me frightened we answer each other's bodies.

Scattered ruins of buildings once grand you have disappeared and all the bells in the house are ringing —

Attackers swarmed forward —

A great white flash

There was nothing more beyond that . . .

There was the man sitting, yes, he was staring into my eyes, I was seeing it through the eyes of another. He seemed to be me . . . a child, it seemed to be you as a child walking . . ." The man you were was looking at you" . . . And who was the "I" sat down suddenly on a park bench, *mal ici*? I watching me. Staring as if through a telescope, how far away . . . I looked straight ahead. Down on a carpet the child. The parents, an interception of the light. A dancing haze of patterns, dreamland until the first orgasm snaps you . . .

Why was I in Paris? To catch a soul . . . feeling the infinite desire for another . . .

"I've been reading your book, *very* dangerous" . . . yes, Mr Green's voice. *"Just get away"* he stated flatly . . .

Spidery, barely legible handwriting . . .

The compartments are moving forward . . . a porthole here and there . . . Is it a Whelme in his room in an empty unfurnished space station?

Young man in the train compartment is seen to be Lazare, before he was obliged or at least entitled to change his name

De Train appears to have no passengers at first though inside one of these cages a young man moves forward. He at last sees the compartment. He taps on the window and the light goes, his own age says:

Come in.

They sing, if they can sing, a duet or somesuch . . .

We'll never forget what we'll never forget . . .

(But anyone can write this . . .)

They become frantic and how to get off the train?

We hear it crossing points when the train stops they scramble . . . and somehow the scenery . . . at the back of the stage we see a vista of ruined houses distant crumbling forts wasteland tossing in the sea our two heroes have disappeared into the wings . . .

Dream voices only beyond this point . . .

My name, come in mine, cling to each other, groan, it seems to be cold and the morning ruined my name . . .

Farms, hammadas, etc, with us again . . . they gaze at a ruined hammada.

In every name remembered in the night, *Vogue says . . .*

They plunge into the outside world . . . stand at the front of the stage, handcuffed together, and speak (or sing):

We're going home as DPPs *(Displaced Persons)*
We need no cash
Going home
And it's awful, unheard of
Indignities, indignities
the terrible indignities!

Vividness, a shining white plane rising in the total blackness in takeoff

Fog

"   only *one* of you!   "

How positively parochial. Did I write that? Time healed the awful delay and killed. A postcard on the desk: *No more extra time.* How long

I've been here and God another call from Mr Green . . ."My dear! I'm so glad to hear you playing for time!" Finally intothe fire, question of getting back. So we were subjected to all manner of threats . . . Holy junk along the boulevard, condescending, manipulating, loveable, on the job . . . Mr Green's mouth twists . . . Wax dolls, stuck through with pins . . . concerted psychic attack entered the apartment. ("Just take this to the apartment on rue St Lazare . . .") What are they all muttering over their dolls, in Time, not too inconspicuously? – Take your cheap naked grandmother to Hell Walk – They all scream: *Dirt*!

Time squirms. Years of victory and devastation.

The infinite loneliness I awake lying on cold hard boards, totally alone at the house staring down at the dark expanse of woodland. Then we were together in the dark, looking back, scattered ruins and I knew we were all spirits. *On est tres mal ici.*

THROUGH THE FEAR

Wrapped in an old black YSL plastic raincoat, waiting, face gaunt, masklike. A lone moment in the universe. Irish coffee on the table in front of him.

Surrounding faces have no meaning for him   no boys, no Old Man, no Bedaya, no Vogue, no Madame Ba, no Windbag, no Mr Green, no KJ

has the Fox got his tail wet? What does he now remember of Chateau-Rouge? And what did he ever? We have heard what he remembers. Precious little. Which may even so be too much for his own good. It was attacked. When? Some Time.

There are very few of us left.

"The man steels himself to endure in hell's provinces . . ."

Trying to make some notes about the drug IANA, but hard to focus . . . . you are lying on a mat . . . the admixture put into the dark . . . a few members left among the stones and the leaves of B . . . apt to be some distance   always away from the village . . . In the darkness and the leaves . . . Recent studies have shown that stillness . . . that voice hovers . . . coming now from beyond your feet, so characteristic of B . . . your very ears, now distant . . . your body lies in darkness, heavy as mine . . . it is this alkaloid that increases the lead . . . coming not seen . . . the ejaculations act as this inhibiter . . . they leave the hut with the speed of thought . . . seeing and hearing appear as one here at the boundary of dead and living . . ." poised in space, a disembodied eye, invisible, incorporeal, seeing but not seen" . . . the man from nowhere is far away.

Like the man with the money.

Endless wait for bread supposed to arrive with some Irishman,

"Andrew," or something, staying at the Tara Hotel. Beginning to doubt the existence of Andrew.

Someone walks over, drops a small note onto the table and leaves. Two telephone numbers and a name.

His head jerks instinctively around to the next table. A sinister trio eyes him closely. Two very creepy middleaged queens and a woman of icily indeterminate age, a sly, chilling, neurotic stare.

One of the queens suddenly seems to ignite spontaneously. He leaps to his feet and lurches over, shockwaves of benevolence and ecstacy blasting Lazare back into his seat in horror.

"You poor *thing*!" the creature shrieks. He looks deeply into Lazare's eyes knowing and loving him through and through. "I *know* what you're going through! I *do*! I *do*! You've been let down, haven't you? *Betrayed*, haven't you?

"Oh, I *know!* I've been through it all! You've known him for years and he's *BETRAYED* you hasn't he *BUT REMEMBER* there are *PEOPLE* here" — he sweeps out his left arm nearly decapitating a passing barman — "there are *PEOPLE*, who are just *here* — HERE! — to *HELP!* — I **know**! — I *know*!" — he is burbling almost sobbing with sincerity — he flops forward over the table wrapping his arms around Lazare — "My friends and I — we KNOW" — Lazare averts his face to one side in the direction of the Friends. They are staring intently — *"COME WITH US! — DON'T LET HIM DESTROY YOU! — DON'T! — DON'T!* —" He is really *glowing*, eyes moist, yearning, beatific.

"You're a good operator. But it doesn't work."

For a few seconds this glowing persona is clouded by sheer pain, then it straightens up and stands back, smiling benignly, knowingly.

Lazare rises: "Take care — you'll need to" he whispers into his ear. "I *know*."

KJ on the line. "The pressure is really on, Jim."

"Yeah, yeah, I know. No problem, no problem, everything's okay."

Maybe.

Reports KJ under arrest in Spain after billion dollar dope bust. Cops confirm and then deny.

KJ on line. Everything okay.

"Better the Welsh rarebit than the Fox. Now Oldfield's bumboy is yesterday's man."

Facility on the line. "I really *must* contact KJ." Can she and Wolf come around to talk? No. How can she contact KJ? No idea. (Jukebox: "*She got a floating bracelet, green eyes and gabby breath*")

Scylla to the right, Charybdis to the left. Or vice versa as the case may be.

How to continue?

Sift, colleague, it's a case of trying . . .

Alternately radiant and dead . . . You were expecting me, once . . . I smiled. Well, they posed as reporter-designer-writer-painter . . . Yes, as I sit here smoking sweet infancy, limitless and frightening . . . We are so short of *people* . . . You're talking about another *person*, you've been here before . . . ?   You're the one who brought fish in

Lifeless terminal existence in London apartment, St Lazare is empty, barren where the soft step forward in human thought drew in the nets . . . the land of the dead lies exotic, radiant and dead. Faced with the prospect of galaxies, do you have *any* idea what it is, the brain? . . . When the spirit's lost and mighty. Bring on the frightened for several ultimately moving targets. Give bones to jellyfish. People are leaving us faster than I stirred my coffee listlessly. I frowned, like an incubus that was forgotten or dissociated, I shrugged. Appearances can be deceptive. I twisted my mouth a little.

"All they have to do is remember"   the Old Man.

I remember it . . .

"I presume there's some reason we want out . . ."

"That's what we're talking about . . ."

135 rue St Martin, the flickering room, breathing mosaics with Bedaya and the Old Man I was saying something like "It's so obvious

right there in front of your eyes" and he was staring back paralysing word and thought and he suddenly thrust his chop-finger right up in front of my eyes — "Remember THAT?" — I felt dizzy, almost nauseous mosaics explode on the wall Paris is swimming — *"THAT!"* — he snapped his fingers. Death. I shivered.

And of course I remember practically nothing. I saw a tossing blue sea in front of me as if projected onto a movie screen and then I lost all sense of division between myself and the screen and was swept along by some uncontrollable volitionary force from one infinitely inconceivable metamorphosis to another a cosmic Disneyland of mock horror certainly enough to damage a child's spirit or send Foutaise flipping right back to the nuthouse, but all so familiar and I realised I was remembering and that I knew this awe-inspiring but somewhat tiresome area very well, I simply — since I had no choice — experienced everything and waited for the next impossibility

Ploughing through solid material a cavern a hall of mirrors —

"Oh no, not the mirrors again!" I groaned — one after another reflecting nothing on and on and on sexually attacked by all manner of quasi-human creatures I could feel no fear except the fear of having no fear I was tired I realised just how exhausting, debilitating all this was I tried to summon my strongest physical fear — of heights — vertigo to break the spell and take refuge in the fear and I was suspended in space like Nelson on his column a whole city spread out below like a relief map and I felt no fear. The movie screen again a bed of green grass and I was back on earth.

— A vertiginous landing strip, coming toward us . . .

ARE YOU INSIDE ME?

Into the centre another phantasmagoria hard to focus a towering structure over the city When we landed we were together re-entry problems you were close then further and further away and you said to come towards you and I tried and went slowly down, rocks, the moving knights and actors Nelson presides rigid down down and switched off no reason to stay up *"Stay up!"* everything transparent and high up and around the walls of vertigo foggy or frighteningly vivid alarmingly fluctuating a street has disappeared I see him pass abject exhaustion alone flooded is my name taxis fly forward another world the days float by until I am pulled out of the water floating face downward my eyes in Paris staring through my hair

"Welcome to the International Boulevard."
"Are you inside me . . . ? My brain is wet . . ."
"*Be!* Stomp your feet!"
I stomped my feet in pain.
"Thank you."
"A pleasure."

We were staying at the waterfront hotel. Bedaya had just left. One of the boys appeared in the doorway and threw in the key and it danced all over the carpet I ran out into the square and howled for Bedaya, he must be very close, howling at a painting nobody could hear. I ran back to the hotel and we searched for the key. It was nowhere to be seen. We tried to pinpoint the area where it had finally come to rest. Then it abruptly reappeared in the centre of the carpet as if it had always been there. An old wireless was making an awful noise. I tried to switch it off or adjust it and then the wireless and the whole room started to mutate incomprehensibly —

"OUT of here!" I shouted.

We just about made it out while the door was still a door.

Bedaya was obviously very close.

But I begin to settle down into the apartment. It is on the ground floor and what I like is that there is no view of anything, unless I want it. The windows are covered. It is quiet and sunny. Occasionally I hear voices from outside and workmen come in to adjust or service this or that piece of apparatus. I have no idea what they are doing. They are very easy and I wander from room to room in dark glasses. The mirror still has a tendency to go into convulsions when I look into it. The key is on the floor.

Bedaya briefly located.

He is having a busy time, many others to deal with, you amongst them. The countryside around here is beautiful. He was finally sitting alone on a bench and I walked up to him.

"Do you have time for me now?" I asked, smiling, expecting the answer.

"*No, no, no . . .*"

"Okay."

He looked up at me.

"We'll have to set ourselves aside a day together . . ." He was tired.

I sat down and put my hand on his shoulder. He smiled and kissed me on the cheek.

"He's a sweet guy, but you can't worry yourself anymore about him . . . either he will or he won't . . ."

Don't know whether it is day or night . . .

Yes it seemed like a hotel, quiet and sunny at first. Occasionally I hear unspoken period when we are voices from outside. We have arrived here at the boundary of dead and living to become clothed with the heavens, the goal of full reception. The heart will be here in a few minutes.

I walked quickly back to the house now it was mid-afternoon. Into the house holding onto my blank whispers.

A sudden ominous half light.

"What's *this*?" I mumbled walking over to the window.

"My ass! *Snow!*" I shivered in disgust.

The phone chirrups like an angry bird.

"How am I? Well, I'm freezing cold, eaten nothing but toast for two days and no more bread left, diagnosed as having ME the post-viral syndrome causing total exhaustion dizziness aches pain weakness in the muscles and joints difficulty in focusing digestive upsets when there's nothing to digest athlete's foot temporary loss of memory and practically any other symptom you like to imagine (Charing Cross Hospital says there's no such thing as ME, maybe they're all Buddhists) Betrayed by my friends that sonofabitching KJ, not to mention you and the I Ching gives out Hexagram 23 *Collapse*."

"Say something different."

"Look you asked and "

"Say something different!"

"What d' "

"Say something *different!*"

(Gleaming sadomasochistic malice and bitchery in your eyes and voice.)

"*Look* "

"Say something DIFFERENT!"

"*Okay*!" I practically screamed. "*FUCK YOU!*"

The haunted Lazare . . .

"*Yeah?*"

Another call from the boys. They seated themselves and I started to give them a rundown on my current operational problems.

"You can't criticize anybody but yourself."

"Yeah . . ."

"You've landed yourself with a lady *Ka! Hah!*" the younger boy taunted, "*My candle burns at both its ends / It will not last the night . .*" He swept a hand through my hair: "You should keep that mess between your legs!" He exploded in maniacal giggles.

Before even I could react the older boy whirled around and slapped him viciously.

"Shut your mouth, you idiot!" he shouted.

The young boy leapt up from the bed burning like a wildcat, eyes blazing.

I walked off into the other room and left them to it, angrily picking up the phone but it was dead.

They were yelling at each other in the next room. I tried the phone again slammed it down burst in and roared at them:

"*If you think things have been tough in the past you ain't seen nothing YET!*"

They both stared, open mouthed, appalled —

I jumped back to the other room, to the mirror.

There was a burning red glow around my hair as if my head was on fire. For a split second I saw Bedaya's face instead of mine.

Had they set up that situation to shift my consciousness? I supposed . . . And yet they had seemed genuinely awestruck by the result. Whatever that was.

Menacing bobs of light danced on the street in front of me.

Met the Old Man at a basement cafe but I can't remember a word of our conversation. We got up to leave, still talking. The area around the counter was crowded and I couldn't catch what he said. I fumbled with my money looked up and he was gone. I pushed my way through the door to the street but he was nowhere in sight.

Pepe and I had the good fortune to be stopped by cops while in the company of Mr Green.

"We've been attending a *vernissage*" Murray drawls.

They look blank.

"A gallery opening, an exhibition of some very fine watercolourists, dating back to the 1940s, who pioneered a "

"What did you say your name was . . . *Sir*?" the cop interjects.

"Smithe, with an eeeeee T H E not Smythe S M Y T H E, who was in fact quite well represented, he was one of our finest colourists with the most exquisite line, he developed a technique whereby "

"Look, we're not much interested in the doings of Mr Smythe, but "

"*AH!* That was Smythe's fate! There was never any interest in him. It broke him. He "

Bristling, the cop starts slapping Pepe's pockets around and rummaging in his bag. He asks him what he does.

"A photographer."

"*Ahh!*" Murray sweeps in " the relationship between painting and photography, a fascinating area, the advent of the camera of course signalled the demise of representation well you know all about that my dear and "

Eyes numbed with incomprehension the dumb cowfaced policewoman looks as if she is facing a firing squad.

" *Now*, the essential point of *choiseisme* "

After about ten minutes of this onslaught they are in full retreat.

"*Poor* Smythe . . ." Murray mumbles to himself.

At Mr Green's insistence I threw away a sharp dangerous kitchen knife given me by Facility.

KJ's contact finally shows up, leaving some kinda Irish cheque which can't be cashed for about three weeks, if at all . . .

KJ on the phone the next day says he will exhibit Bedaya's last Big Picture at this Arabic event in Paris this summer. Said he was off to the Middle East — word is that someone tried to kill him at R's place on the Quai — bullet through the window —

"They're trynah deprive me of my chivil liberties̲h!"

— Flash of KJ trailing diplomatic plates, codenames, false passports, dummy corporations, a wallet almost as big as his mouth — ("Nothing is true") —

"Uh, what's this these are Frog photographers? — ah, right — ah, Je, KJ McCann — ah — wha — ? — this sonofabitching thing's not workin — gimme that fuckin mike — KJ McCann and I have somethin to say to you, Old Man, Vogue/Whelme/Lazare or whatever your fuckin name is I pledge myself against the imperialisht onslaught of international Zionism, Friends of Bedaya . . . Keeni Meenis . . . I know who it is . . . the unholy trinity again . . . the Brits . . . bureaucracy . . . Old Man your psychic kneecaps . . . should be blown off . . . CIA . . . thought control and smack distribution agent . . ."

(So why did I take this money from KJ? Well, being influenced by the works of Hassan i Sabbah and aiming to live my life as an ongoing diarrhoea of bullshit, with style, I had this connection — wait for this — with this group of Islamic fundamentalists, so I intended to arm them — these fundamentalists that is — (*God,* what shit) — overthrowing the Moroccan government in my spare time . . .)

Paris gets on my nerves these days, full of enemies . . .

— (I arrived back at the apartment mid-afternoon, to be met by stupid hostility . . .)

"Don't you know who you are attacking?" the older boy shouted.

"Who is . . . he . . . attacking?"

"Well, *he* — himself, of course . . ." —

The headquarters of the Psychic Ten, fronted by a restaurant on the Ile St Louis, originally pointed out to me by Bedaya . . . gaunt in his musty mortician's suit, one of the ten men in the world who don't sleep .

. . We are a judicial body. We are *not* associated with the Old Man, Bedaya, Friends of Bedaya, Madame Ba though she has been summoned before us on more than one occasion — KJ McCann, Madame Windhover . . . her least of all . . . (His mouth twists with distaste.)

What is the relationship with the group established by Bedaya?

None.

Some of us have better memories?

(He twitches at the papers on his desk, apparently bored.)

Like a death threat, on one . . . occasion . . .

Death is always threatening us.

No shit.

We do *not* approve of them or of you or of any of your activities. You think you have sought us out . . . You have not, you have been *summoned.*

Exciting. How many times you summoned that Bavarian bitch?

Uh are those papers bothering you?

More than *once* but once will be enough for you.

Yes, yes, but let's not have any more threats of terminal illness, uh?

If the threat is not directed toward him it may be directed toward you.

The last night of the year. They can't afford the rent . . .

Perhaps we would like to know exactly what Bedaya did achieve.

The Old Man once exclaimed that, apart from anything else, Bedaya was one of the greatest painters that ever lived. Well, to be a great painter is one thing.

And what does that entail? *Being there before others, and making it possible for others?*

Maybe as simple as that. Maybe not.

"He comes forth by extracting himself from himself . . ."

Lazare, tracking Bedaya through the wastes of the Inner Hotel . . .

A long dark road, terrible winds, flowers fly past, high in nowhere where I really come from, limitless and frightening my head dropped to my knees *"Stay up!"* battles of the night, vomit and dust losing my time, the senses and I are twisting — I'm going back with him, no more extra time —

— Moss, leaves, vines, clinging to crumbled grandeur — sun on the leaves —

Lazare wanders delirious, soul on fire.

Survivor of his own burial such is his nature: the rising and setting sun.

He had regained his voice, yammering like a demented desert *nabi*.

How to follow the day and overcome despair! Even trees fall!

The flood takes him. The sun takes him. He saw the storm gathering from the north.

Sceptres fall to dust on the riverbank, the Unawakened who lies dead now rising from the tomb — Any evil could possess you! — In shallow water I cause the Other to burst forth casting to the flame that which the soul sustains. In sustaining the shadow I consume the True Source! In you I call forth the Other. Flooded is my name! In this body, which is yours, he comes forth by extracting himself from himself. It's not much fun. I wake the Other, hungry for torment! Penetrate me on that day of trial! — Tears flow! —

Flooded is my name! — slowly down down a closed circle around the rise in the holy barque of Night the movement of eternal Return when you bring your flesh to rest. And thus reach the Beyond — Violence rules all! — Then united we shall form the Abode. Truth above the Law

— Listen to me rotting under the burning sky! — Endure the pain of life. Denying me is acclaimed by the mob! Rapacious are hearts on the shore of ecstacy — Flooded is my name! — Cry out! — Brother, as long as you burn you belong. One is pushed into darkness. He who dwells within, the knower unknown. Virtues of creation, builders like gods —

The room was suffused in an odd spectral light. I lurched to my feet and swept to the window. The blue sheet covering it had partly fallen to the floor. It was as light as day. And there was the Star. Huge. Dazzling.

"*Heaven!*" I murmured, awestruck.

I didn't look at it directly I was pulled back, examining the room, everything in complete disarray, overturned chairs, I floated through the door without opening it the shower was running there hadn't been one before (switching off the heat) I hovered through into the other room knowing I was in future time the same chaos it was now daylight I wanted to see the street outside I ripped down the curtain but the street was unrecognizable . .. construction workers . . . high spiralling clouds . . . hovered like the lost soul's reply

Doctor T! Thousand Fingers!
The high clouds had made it seem easy to talk from the mouth

"You left me alone" he says. Yes, I do, you are a domestic animal and I dream of cutting your balls every morning after two my legs are painful, full of blood! full of things like that happening in my life!

People cut my oxygen! They are stealing my air my precious little atmosphere my ozone and gas! I'm tired of all this! These people, what do they want? they want to drive me insane! I can't stand it! My existence is a nightmare! Dancing like a fool crossing the white grey black and brown silhouettes, small groups, flying coloured shirts hanging, Sida jeans, army blouses and cheap blankets and no one will look at me! Or will they do it in the same time anyway? I did behave badly Wind of the Boulevard is withering outside to the terrace my love, with your one-eyed mind! when will they stop buying cheap blankets army blouses and Sida jeans?

And the wind of the apartment. No order. It's like someone is always needed to put the chairs on the table. And the wind will throw them back on the floor! A man is needed for that! He is a worker! Chateau Rouge is into transformation, again. The Ba Cafe! They make another terrace to preserve it. After they will paint inside and remove the decorations Didn't you like this marvellous feeling to be drinking in the middle of the road? (Paris can't offer it any more) Cops enter and everyone jumps into the back where the waiter is washing his hand like an English tail! (Cover your ass.)

Yeah? another wank from the two boys? They wank themselves and I started to wank them a rundown on my current operational wank you can't criticize wank but yourself yeah, you wank yourself with a lady *Ka*! And as you don't love me anymore you won't forgive . . .

I am here and there a spot on the roof vaguely showing me where I could find me. The spotlight is moving the move is hard to follow, uncontrollable, have got an evil reflecting in the back of my neck I am searching for my soul and I lost my mind doing it. Like music is made for people with no ears. The value of my love is decreasing! And, like the snake, change is skin!

Fight it, the filter! The filter — the machine, the savoir faire, the way!

If I change my machine it will never work again — if it doesn't work I will never have any line in my end! It will be like an ending to something. I already know! Boys and girls, mothers! — will I still look for a father, will I see and feel it like I did when I sleep daytime, it seems so unattractive and a talk with him is so cold — People start to threaten to get back what they have given — no friends anymore! — the only thing I have to do is pay — things don't seem to have been done in a really perfect way. I really don't know what I am living at the moment, I don't know — I seem to remember it, maybe I do — the way of the Scorpion is a rebirth and it could happen in all kinds of ways, even the Supreme Offering to the fire which will never cool. I am crushed with grief from loss of ME! Hearts are rapacious in that stillness. Flooded is my name! (Today is odour of myrrh — dusk nestling among the reeds —)

Flooded is my name! — No end to it! — Worse than flesh rejected from the Pyramids. I spoke to my soul like a shelter from a windy day —

You say you want me with you in the Beyond — Disfigured are faces! The lost man is cast from his house and enacting the miracle of the creator. Consciousness. Deed. Men are pirates. You will stand on the Other Side, upon the hill! See Home after years held in bondage! —

The sun goes down. A single star irradiates the scene.

Flooded temples . . .

He was slapping my face, smiling.

"*What* is your name?"

"Flooded" I mumbled.

"We weren't sure you were coming out of that one . . ."

"I'm not sure I am out of it . . ."

— Bedaya talking, the Old Man nodding in agreement . . .

"You need a new soul down there" — he was staring at my shoe "Do *you* believe in saints?"

"I don't believe in *hotels*, personally" the Old Man intones.

"But this one's a fullblown . . . flooded saint . . ." (choking with laughter)

"Kinda overblown line in delirium for *myyy* taste . . ."

His voice, fading away, rolling a joint . . .

I lurched to my feet

Spring and summer must be prepared — Hope to hear from you soon

(The workmen are here again)

A long dark road splendid but rotting . . . impressively . . . *Hot & Hung* magazines rotting . . . I saw Bedaya again knowing there was little time. I had to leave but it was too late I didn't know what life I am living.

He said the contracts must be *firm*, unbending.

A man comes in and goes out. I am presenting someone who is not here. I am uncomfortable with my ME. Blank post-viral whispers Sudden ominous half dizziness, pain, light

"What's *this*?"

An angry bird chirrups. *There is no such thing as ME!* — and the I Ching screams:

FUCK YOU!

The boys were mumbling slurring their words as if barely able to keep awake. I could hardly speak.

I dragged myself to my feet.

"This is sheer hell" I groaned. "Just to keep my shoes on . . ."

If there was anything to say, nobody had the energy to say it.

I went into the kitchen and made soup out of some kind of nameless fish.

They both stared at it in disbelief. It looked like something out of a diseased liver.

"And what in hell is *that*?"

"It's all there is" T mumbled. "I think it's okay." I filled three mugs. It tasted better than it looked, which was not saying much.

All three of us fell asleep, exhausted.

Back at the apartment I leaf through *Hot & Hung* and *Pleasant Life* . . .

"'Dirk doted on Diamante and they would often retreat to Wiltshire . . . . (Dead leaves . . . ashes . . .)'"

"'It's so divine to roll a joint on Paris *Vogue*, 1961. This house is everything we ever wanted. Children are good for the Place . . .'"

— The human race for death — make me karma — the water is still there and swimming the tide is lies — people walking in every direction

"Are you coming?" (they have all lost their shoes)

The duchess glanced at Murray Limpwell's feet with disapproval.

"Can't you go any faster than this?"

"No!" Murray said. Faintly.

"What's *wrong*?"

"Oh, just a tiny spot of heart trouble."

"We *all* have it!" snapped Facility.

Fuming at the characteristically patronising tone, Murray went a shade slower.

"Are you coming?"

"Yes, we must push on . . . this street *is* awfully dark."

"Oh, rubbish! What *is* wrong with you."

"Dissimilar disrhythm."

Facility seemed dazed.

"Never heard of it."

Murray said it again.

"DISSIMILAR DISRHYTHM."

"Odd" Facility said.

"It just means" Murray said patiently, "I have to go *slowly* . . ."

Human consciousness is to be extirpated. You live by night and I hardly live at all. Howling dogs a terrible impasse . . . We were so turned on . . .

Bedaya close and closer more and more solid I regard my present life as that which was given me by him I can't stand it! Haunted, flooded, thousand fingered, Lazare, sinking and swimming . . .

"You don't want to cry as long as you have the strength "

He sits back from the typewriter.

Time . . . us again. It is the land of this perilous passage to a distant star, that long long way we have to be stronger. I love courage when you want to stay to wait for it to be stronger delicate spirits wild that can be everything we decide. Write my book for me. I can arrange a single star, hovering . . . a delicate door open, a tract for you. Out of the past. I am speechless, returning to the story we don't exactly remember, at night, trying to find what we have, remember exactly what it was, a kind of night. Candles, ruined staircases of the chateau. We entered the room lost do we know when? A bare empty room with skylight, *irradiated* we were both waiting for it to be a bridge even though you always pay creating a bridge And many are crossing it their star their bridge to the Other. There it was like a world burning in the sky. Honestly you could make windows break Our lesson will be to arrive where

Everything you say can be reversed, I said. One day the Blue Virgin enters the room destroying everything explodes and crashes to the ground, her staff dressed in blue conjurers will always drop in turning my gaze fixed frozen whole building starts to explode the window in all its glory *Keep looking!* Be as cautious as you can, of course, about enhancing your position. Whatever left of it hasn't been siphoned . . . you know, as soon as you have anything like a kingdom . . .

Who *are* these people? *Where are you?*

"Where are we now?" Facility asked brightly, swinging to the play like one of the ladies of St James's.

"We're near the rue de l'Offensif."

"*Where?*"

Softly, softly, I could hardly drag myself down into the feeling of utter doom, the rue de l'Offensif swaying. And you, naturally enough . . . here. Less empty every day — He was slapping my face — A canvas, your apartment and apartment block I knew it was the passage, the whole market in my nerves — terribly wanting — the canvas is coming alive — In you I woke up to the smell of dried vomit and with more and more writhing voodoo goddesses something that at first looked onto the bed — Yeah, I've lived here with the Blue Virgin on me, I said. There was a note on your door with the huge empty canvas, great, white —

NO MORE EXTRA TIME!

I opened my eyes looked out and the great glass door suddenly exploded the French window crashes to smithereens a blinding flash

The young boy walking hurriedly for the train dodging cops through the Arab market turns abruptly is struck by a crushing force and wakes in the arms of the Other

"Are you *coming*?"

"Sure, the door exploded and I plodded on, you know memories after that. The ashtray was moving. On my hands and knees . . . crying . . .

"Murray Green . . . He was staring. Yes, the street yesterday, dying. We're getting close to the end, sure. An old hand. Mistakes are deadly. I stared at the floor. It was sparkling, elegant, the end of the week at least. And who is Mr Green? Yes, I was down on the street it was the cafe terrace, a table. Whatever . . . I was dying . . . I'd like you to find out . . . or help, but no one could see or hear, did I ever leave that door . . . ? You recognized that street yesterday. Crowded. Frighteningly old, congealed. A corner of his mouth twisted along the bar in Pigalle. He frowned. I was staring at the wall. In fact, I smiled. I looked around. Like it was designed by Ba I said. He made a half turn towards me then. He moaned wearily . . . both definitively and ironically. Pickings are the beings trapped here. It has always been . . . To try to change a little? His mouth quivered into a thin grimace, he was obviously consulting an oracle . . . staring deeply . . ."

We had fought our way through. Survived the shattering onslaught

The Star hovers . . .

"We're going back?"
"Yes, it's over . . ."

Survived and describing . . . the sun, remember it suddenly like spring exhilarating . . . If he got out, I don't know. You were playing for Time, *he* wouldn't. He had no time left. It was too late. Why should they ever reply to his Earl Grey? It's The Spot. He was nearly 80. That type. We all hope for other places . . . minds of our readers . . .

They approached a light, an increasingly diminutive Murray crawling gently along, Facility trying to look neither too tall nor too bulky. She fitted her pace to his.

"Look, Murray, it says rue de *l'Assomption*!"

"Oh, yes, of course. It's going up in the world."

"Do be careful how you walk. I don't want you falling over, Murray."

"No. All right."

Facility took a deep breath. "Look. Isn't that a bus stop?"

"It's in the dark."

"Oh, I'll wait there. You go on."

"I can't let you stand there, Facility."

"Yes you can."

"But you'd be mugged. You'd be *asking* for it."

"Oh, I don't mind."

"No, Facility, I'll take you to the next stop. It'll be safer."

They lumbered along together.

"You're so lucky! Really Murray, you'll have such a comfortable death!"

As I walked back clouds were forming Mr Green. Cane, raincoat draped over his arm, they got to me before you did . . . beautiful manners in the old style floating in the sky, dapper, willowy, old gentleman, suit, tie, *Au revoir*, Mr Green I said. He was staring . . . ? He drifted languidly, over . . .

The man from nowhere is trying to make some notes about the drug, you are lying on a mat.

A telephone on the bed. You pick up the receiver and dial a number. No reply. I pick up the receiver put it to my ear and then slam it down in a parody of agitation, smiling. Bedaya lay back on the bed with his notes. We caressed a little at the foot of the bed, falling asleep on the mat.

Later Bedaya was up and so was I. You were still asleep on the mat.

"Let him rest. He's okay" Bedaya said.

He turned me around by the shoulders and stared into my eyes.

"Are you ready to work for me again?"

I smiled back.

"Whenever wasn't I?"

"In about ten minutes . . . ?"

Voice fading . . .

Yes. You hear me now? Yes. Yes. Yes, okay . . . *silence crashing* . . . You . . . you have to be very careful. You. I can hear you now. Yes? Yes . . . *crashing crackling* . . . So much opposition . . . to you . . . It's inevitable isn't it . . . ? *Hoarse crackling* . . . No . . . ? Yes. They tried to kill me — *The Voice* — And they tried to kill you. Yes. No, the line is terrible. You. They tried to kill you . . . think: why is there so much opposition? Yes? I can't hear you. No. Yes. Continue by means of the Third, call when it becomes necessary —

You know we intend to

The essence of the *Ka* floats in Irish coffee as the glasses clink together, the beginning of a new age.

THE NERVOUS SYSTEM

For the limit, I am the one . . ."

THE FLAW

(Inevitable Cops)

It has been said of KJ of course that he has no respect for human life. Except his own, of course. Actually this characteristic was originally attributed to another and later applied to KJ.

I remember once on the autobahn babies burning in a sheet of gasoline three cars incinerated, cops, fire brigade, held up there for three hours till they could clear this mess like nothing ever happened, traffic jammed all the way back to Berlin. We stood there smoking, waiting.

"It's very easy to come to terms with other people's deaths," KJ mused philosophically.

I murmured assent.

"Did it really hit *you* when Bedaya died?" he persisted.

"No. Not at first."

"He did rather drag it out a bit."

KJ, like Bedaya, operates an area of the so-called Other Method, which we refer to as the Nervous System. KJ also shares a fatal flaw with Bedaya — it was fatal for Bedaya at any rate — that of insistence on being smarter than anyone else. Of course, Bedaya was smarter than others. The flaw was his increasingly relentless determination to demonstrate it. Insecurity — (KJ disputes all this — noisily. KJ has a problem with security) — But after all it is a Nervous System. A system of stealth.

And this book is therefore written according to its rules . . .

Whelme was an experienced agent — known as Lazare in the trade — who had seen out a number of old pros in his time. His main assignment had been what is known as *changing the cut-outs*. "Cut-outs" is a term like *shoes*, for an agent's cover, that which he needs daily to walk around and function in   cut-outs are strictly *speaking covers* produced by layer upon layer of intensive conditioning. The subject under interrogation will remember this he will remember that will tell you a story of years of training and hard knocks   all these layers are carefully programmed of course   and this could go on forever or at least until somebody finally got to the end of the programming by which time you could probably just as well forget about it.

It is a point to remember   that all Intelligence systems are variants of the same system. Paths which meet and are one. Taught by Bedaya Whelme had used the tehnique known in Islamic traditional programming as *ta'wil*   "to take something (forcibly if necessary) back to its source or deepest significance"   penetration   "The Great Awakening!"   *Ta'wil* is camouflaged by *taqqyyia*   concealment, dissimulation   The Nervous System: *Yek-e bud*   Once there was   *Yek-e nabud*   Once there wasn't. He worked through layers of intensive conditioning.*

So all the players are playing on the same lines but their motives may   rarely   be different. Whelme's assignment was to connect with already conditioned subjects   specific subjects otherwise you could be in there with just about everyone   and shift them around to some position where their activities might be of more use to US, essentially. He worked essentially on the international queer scene, of course, replete with old pederast priests cum concrete poet tarot reading advisers to President Nasser inviting him to Prinknash Abbey. Well, he saw them all out . . .

"*'Cut-outs!'* I said: 'You're *crazy!'*" Paul Bowles is exclaiming.

Tangier 90

It took awhile for us to find the Inmeuble Itesa. We, Philippe Baumont and I, were in Tangier as representatives   or "cultural co-ordinators" as KJ likes to put it   of the fabled European arts foundation the founding father of which (KJ) had just helpfully advised the press that he was funding Islamic fundamentalist tribesmen in an

* P.L. Wilson, *Scandal* (1988) and "Haut Brion" (T.Wilson) in *Man From Nowhere* (1992). I am credited (if that is the word) with co-authoring the latter production. This is unso.

attempt to overthrow the king. As far as we were concerned we were there to arrange a showing of Brion Gysin's last Big Picture, the *Makemono**. Naturally, under the circumstances, we found ourselves subjected to opposition and support from all manner of interested parties . . . . The Moroccan undercover cop out of a Marx Brothers movie — sometimes a moustache, sometimes not — got right onto the job and resorted to poison without further ado. After that, having laid us both out for about 24 hours of continual vomiting, he seemed content to observe comings and goings from the hotel lounge, with or without his moustache. The French and the Americans opened their doors and their ears. Gavin Young was in town.

Also on hand were the incomparable Hamri and, of course, the practically immortal David Herbert. Expected immanently were Ira Cohen, longtime Bowles amigo, and his son Raphael, who were to complete our somewhat motley crew.

Anyway, after we managed to get up off the floor we tottered down the stairs past the cop and out, heading for the Itesa, Calle Campoamor on the western outskirts totally nondescript, totally anonymous, this is the way, all the way up to the top floor. There is no phone. You just drop around. I give the door a tap and a couple of raps eventually it opens and Mrabet, small, poker-faced, wiry, somnolent, lets us in. Through the foyer stacked high with leather suitcases and trunks and into the salon. I have with me a Swedish magazine with Bowles interview I imagine Paul may not have seen but he has and immediately launches into a complaint about the interviewer who has apparently also broken into print expressing dismay at the austerity of the Bowles living conditions.

Paul is not amused, as if somehow I am responsible. This is amusing since the same writer had previously given my place the once-over . . "the mysteriously bulging walls, the permanent deep chill no heater can quite dispel" . . . etc. Paul has about three and a half rooms up there. No doubt Howard Hughes would have found it a bit hairy, but he is quite comfortable. He has lived in this apartment since the late fifties and in Tangier of course longer than practically anyone, with the exception of Lord David I suppose.

**Calligraffiti of Fire*, 1985

Paul was generally confined to bed during the period of our visit and was more or less content, especially after Ira arrived, to sit back and listen, frail, white-haired, bright-eyed, benignly bemused . . . We talk about Brion as the apartment slowly fills up as it does every day, these days, with a succession of camera crews, journalists, old friends, new friends, when someone remarks on Paul's apparent light-heartedness he smiles back, "That's because I'm in pain." A typical Bowles response. Ira says that when he asked Paul why he wrote his poignant and obviously deeply-felt poem 'Next to Nothing' (originally published by Ira in Nepal) he replied: "Because you asked me." The old names hover in the air . . . Brion . . . Alfred . . . Yacoubi . . . Sherifa, Jane, "existing only in the minds of us who remember . . ." The lights flicker I amble back through the smoky salon to find Mrabet locked eyeball to dilated eyeball with a fat young American filmmaker, a confrontation between Fu Manchu and Humpty Dumpty. "At least his first few little cheques were good" Mrabet seems to be rasping. Back into the bedroom, Phillip Ramey is there, Abdelouahid, Paul's driver, Raphael, Ira . . . "*Truman*" . . . "*Alfred*" . . "*Yacoubi*" . . . "*Jane*" . . . "*Sherifa*" . . . "*Brion*" . . .

"And when our lines have been cut as well, we shall all be a part of the same *grand neant*. Even that consoling thought isn't of much help." (PB)

The lights have blown but the names still hover . . .

Bedaya, Man From Nowhere, a stricken mage who has left behind a sink-or-swim legacy to his disputive team of followers.

A young man, typing the story, remembering the perilous passage. Or doing his best, "returning to the story we don't exactly remember . . ." Another vague, shadowy figure, dialogue is eliptical, disconnected "you better write my book for me" a huge single star hovers, irradiating the room . . ."Our lesson will be to arrive where we started this magic melts slowly in us again . . ." They have taken a drug to assist them.

Arriving where he started, which appears to be Paris, the young man meets his contact, stirring his coffee listlessly, facing the music . . ."You seem to have managed a total fuckup." Dialogue has the same mysterious quality as before . . . ("The Old Man and I drew in the nets . . .") and again the figures are shadowy. Street scenes London, Paris, etc flash by . . ." This is the past between mosaics . . ." A woodland scene at night — spectral ruins — Bedaya and others appear. The meeting is disrupted by costumed attackers and we all retreat.

I made it easily through customs and found a cab.

An envelope containing about £700 expenses and more disembodied conversation . . . gaining or losing "power in this world . . ."

Mr Green, "an old hand" is on his trail. Mr Green, whose message, essentially, is that he should get out of Paris, fast. Bedaya's strategy. Who actually paid the expenses?

More encounters with Mr Green, whose attempts to warn him off have an increasing sense of urgency — hallucinatory explosions of long buried memory — *on est tres mal ici* — Travelling through these friendless wastes. Sun on my back. A dazzling sign. Walking through snow, much younger. Satchel over my shoulder. Sadness that I am not really *here* . . . knowing then what I know now. I remember riding my bike home along Crow Green Road and falling off at the corner of sunset and Orchard Lane spraining my wrist. I walked the bike back and my mother put my arm in a sling and I went to bed. An aching sleepless night. I finally got up and walked through to the lounge sleeping fitfully on the sofa and then the heavenly light came in through the french windows and the leaves as I lay there and my mother and father came in and he drove me to the nearest hospital through the dazzling sun and leaves of lost Saturday light the pain was gone

"Feeling no pain?" Jim says, staring ahead, steering through blinding snow . . .

We thought *he* could never take over from Bedaya. But he did, all the way back into the can. A driven man — *Look out!* —

The Third Mind — "subjected to threats and support from all manner of interested parties" — which has survived a shattering onslaught — and Bedaya's death.

"No more extra time" (Bedaya's voice)

Fire

The hamman. 4 a.m. A hoarse whispering voice . . . "Hassan i Sabbah's programme?" . . . *"You hear me now?"* — Devastation of opposition parties, "maintainers of false consciousness" — Wax dolls. The world on fire — KJ, cultural incendiarist whose cover is colourful international fabulist-prankster . . . (Vatican vernissage. Pope nearly dies of heart failure as he unveils lurid triptych depicting animal sex. KJ has switched the exhibits. The original "Sacred Art" is now in his safekeeping . . .) Concerted psychic attack. The fire . . . The fear of really *"What are you doing?"* approaching the Pain Barrier and passing through it

And we certainly had all the rats on our tail from Paris to Strasbourg to Rotterdam, Amsterdam, Tangier, Berlin and back KJ continually, convulsively, backtracking, sidetripping, spreading a minefield of misinformation across Europe and North Africa like a human hurricane

"DON'T PANIC BROTHER! Everything's under control!

I've planned everyth *FUUUUUUCK!* "

The phone goes dead.

Us again . . . in the world of KJ . . .

Look-What-I-Did is outlining his supposed projects and predelictions with maniacal indiscretion in a crowded bar The floor is his.

"We have no pity, we have guns and we know how to use them!" "Look what I did to the centre of Belfast! " " Do *I* know how to wash money? *Is the Pope Polish?"*

Madness is his Method.

"Now this is a high security operation and I don't want you getting out of control!" jabbing his finger at me *"No fuckups!* We play it *cool DISCREET! Garcon! GEMME A FUCKIN DRINK!* "

At the next table some kind of French intellectual type trying to read something and not scream at the same time reaches out for his beer which is instantly swept off by KJ who is pausing for five seconds

KJ came in late in my story, much later than Bedaya, Vogue or the Old Man of whom I've written. The premise of these practitioners of the Unsafe (we are extending KJ's five seconds under loud protest) was that the world *as we perceive it* is produced by a single obsessive act sexual union between male and female. Union between those of the same sex does not reproduce human time in that way. So that was one aspect of the Other Method. Along with the use of drugs, powerful mind-changing and hopefully educational agents. A third was the Nervous System of behaviour.

KJ is haranguing the entire bar

"— *Frogs! — camel-jockeys! — spaghetti-benders! — Hebes!* — "

He homes in on a table which is being swiftly — but not swiftly enough — evacuated by two elegant young fashion fags and a female Javanese midget.

The Garb Age. All these boys and their ersatz girlfriends — Jacky and Jane out of the Velvet Underground travelling aimlessly around. Dedicated agents, looking for music. A bit much.

"WHAT IS THE NATURE OF LOVE?" he demands, almost knocking her teeth out with his forefinger.

The trio backs slowly away with synchronised catlike steps, hotly pursued by KJ — "I remember when I was in India and I was in love with this elephant — " (Jima Khan has taken over momentarily — *control him!*) — " — it was the annual elephant round-up — an I used to go out an every time I saw this fuckin elephant I was — " He makes vigorously explicit gestures to illustrate his point.

We are moving to another hotel — (we do this a lot. For security reasons) — under my name, KJ as my assistant. KJ immediately has the manager cornered behind his desk hoarsely whispering "I really hope Mr Whelme doesn't throw one of his wild parties! — I'll try, I'll try but he's so, so dominating and really — how to say — *irrational*, sometimes! *It's impossible to control him*! It's a very sad case but I'll — *LOOK OUT! — he's coming down the* — "

After one of Mr Whelme's parties — in the course of which so many frantic whores, dealers, designers, a team of morticians and a supposed elephant tamer known as Samy the Leb went up and down in the elevator it finally gave up halfway with several of these characters and the assistant manager of the hotel trapped inside — we were informed that the place was now fully booked until the end of the century at least as far as KJ is concerned.

As can be seen, judging by his public appearances, KJ is either a consumate practitioner of the Nervous System, or he is quite mad. Perhaps both. Nobody has ever been able to work it out.

Wax dolls. The world on fire. Concerted psychic attack. Fire ahead. The Chateau, a training establishment operated by Bedaya, and the other boys. "It's difficult to know if this is happening now or if I am remembering. Maybe both . . . We were being trained . . ."

Travel   the past   Where are we now?

Well . . . snow . . . '86-'87, we were on our way to someplace on the French-Belgian border where Kj was leaving me for the weekend with some personality who apparently has   or has access to   a copy of the long-lost Beckett manuscript *Once Thought No Longer.* The title speaks for itself, I think sourly.

"So he has this manuscript?"

"*We* have it."

"Uh . . ."

"Beckett will do what I tell him to do."

"Good."

KJ is plowing through the autobahn like the chariot race in *Ben Hur* cool, calm, no *Get the fuck outta my way*!   But they do, pretty fast.

"*I have lost my gun and nothing to eat and Indians hunting me*, Ezra Kind carved onto the so-called Thoen Stone and died, sooner or later." Our man is it seems an authority on whatever there is to be an authority about . . . A slab of rock in Spearfish, South Dakota.

"Came to these hills in 1833, seven of us" he recited   *"Delacompt, Ezra Kind, G.W. Wood, T. Brown, R. Kent, Wm King, Indian Crow   all dead but me, Ezra Kind. Got our gold June. Got all the gold we could carry. Our ponies all got by Indians. I have lost my gun and nothing to eat and Indians hunting me* . . . Their remains were never found."

He smiled, mid-sixties kind of Greek who makes his own taramasalata he could be an art dealer a book dealer any kind of dealer. Every kind in his time no doubt. Remains never found.

"Is anybody particularly looking for them?"

"Will you take another sherry?"

"Thank you."

He brought it, referring me to the standard work on the subject, *Last Buffalo of the Black Hills.*

"I know. I reviewed it once" I said,* hopefully cutting short the saga of Spearfish. I felt sure KJ had put him up to all this guff.

**Last Buffalo of the Black Hills* by Frank Thomson, reviewed in *The Tally Sheet,* London, circa 1963

He sat down again.

"And how do you feel about the Lost Dutchman?"

"I figure the Superstition Mountains are welcome to him" I sighed. "How do you feel about Beckett?"

(The Lost Dutchman was some kind of extended old Western in the Superstition Mountains God knows where, a Dutch prospector allegedly struck it rich and disappeared. Various other nationalities repeatedly followed over the decades and met the same fate or eventually staggered back out of the hills in states of terminal delirium. All this apparently went on up to the turn of the century or beyond until the original inhabitants of this supposedly sacred area and everyone else finally gave up on the whole situation . . .)

"I understand he's not very well."

"There's this manuscript?"

"Oh, a manuscript, yes, interesting idea . . ."

"A story told by a person who can't remember the story, it seems . . ."

I smiled. "Old trick. Lost my gun, nothing to eat . . ."

He smiled back. "Yes, rather truncated. Another sherry?"

He poured it.

"And what of our friend KJ's projects these days?"

"He's into art."

He laughed pleasantly. It was the morning.

"Ah, yes, he is an artist. A great artist."

He laughed some more, an engaging man.

"How does he do it? Because they do not want to *cannot* break the spell. They have to believe. He is so strong . . . The writer, cannot *write* a happy ending. He can produce a positive, constructive script but the end must always be tentative, wanting . . . Fighting . . . until there is no more fight left. Just life . . . I remember drinking something in a cafe in Montmartre at seven in the morning" . . . he gestured . . . "Sacre Coeur up there . . . lost . . . You think, originally, I am blessed by the fact of this inimitable knowledge I am passing on. But you are cursed . . . lost . . ."

A silence.

"By the way, I am not Greek, as I may have given the impression . . . I am Dutch."

I went up to my bedroom neither knowing nor caring whether he had a copy of this manuscript or had ever seen one.

Flashes of Bedaya as beachboy, painter, agent, restaurateur, etc Tangier scenes from old movies seedy operators in the Socco Chico Fire illuminates the sign: 1001 NIGHTS on an ancient wooden door which slowly opens to spectacular scene: trance musicians, dancing-boys, fire-eaters, same seedy operators conspire around the huge open log fire the menu is *burnt* onto a wooden tablet "Quick! It's alive! *Eat it!*" The Other Method up for grabs Facility, Duchess of Wind (British Intelligence) chased from Morocco to Paris meeting with the Old Man the two maverick agents mount Operation Rewrite using Hassan i Sabbah as a model. "Putting themselves together at hazard" cut-ups self-explained the third and superior mind disrupting the control lines via minds of others worldwide ("The Old Man and I drew in the nets")

"An experiment which failed, but which is still going on . . ."

"Oh, Jesus Christ!" The Lost Dutchman permitted himself a rare profanity. An autumn fire crackled away mangled and contorted.

"They think, now, that they have found a new cause of Death, but what kills us has always killed us . . . The only difficulties involved are those left here. Those who *have* left may have their own problems . . ."

I looked up.

He sighed a little and poked the fire maliciously a log buckled and snapped as I stared fascinated.

"Um . . . I was trying to remember something . ." He was reciting again . . . "*It's only me thinking about it. Is anyone else thinking about it? Who is anyone else? Once thought no longer . . .*"

"*Do* you have this manuscript?"

"I think I saw it once . . . KJ said it was in my possession?"

"Yes."

"Hmm. Well at least it would have been safer with me than with him . . ."

"Too bad." I smiled.

"I find it unreadable, personally."

"At least not long."

"It has that merit . . . If you're going in for distinctions like that . . ."

"Hmm." I picked up the poker and started agitating the fire. I felt a little unsure as to which manuscript it was under discussion.

"I'm heading for an overload," I said after a long silence.

"I think you've already had one. A major reversal. A loss, a quite considerable loss. A life-threatening situation. Naturally you're shaken."

It's just when I think of the effort, the commitment, that went into all this, after such a period of time . . .

"Yes. Well, the manuscript was just a ploy . . . So you wouldn't be *entirely* on your own . . ."

Staying power, just about shot, like the fire, the whole fucking burning world, the hole in the heart's affections. Incinerated chicken bones. The fire went wild.

Scenes from London period, heavy, oppressive . . . "They do not always remember . . ." Terror at Alamut — (He had always liked to be scared: addicted to terror the stricken mage) — another collaboration — extending the chain — Parasites move in — Friends of Bedaya, Inc. — (unctuous American voiceover here: "We confidently expect to see the Third Mind relegated to the archives . . . most profitably . . .) —

An insane mix of rhythm and melody, ranting voices car alarms police sirens dog fights and pneumatic drills — several earlier scenes cut into each other — Mist drifts over the river. They scramble down to the white stone village, La Roche-Guyon, far away.

Sitting smoking in the mirror . . . fisherman drawing in nets . . . ?

Time to go. I had a train to catch, yet another. I shared a compartment with a homely old couple I took to be Austrian or somesuch. They didn't say a word to each other. I gave a start when after about twenty minutes the woman sat forward:

"EXCUSE ME, can you help? My husband's legs are very bad. The cases . . ."

English? I wasn't aware there was a stop due. Well, I humped half of their baggage out into the corridor people pushing and shoving behind us the train still not stopping I dropped the stuff suddenly and turned faced by three unmistakable dark suits and ties "Through into here sir, please" more English. Another suit was helping the couple with their bags. They looked at me, blank faced.

We sat there in the compartment, the four of us, saying nothing.

Finally I asked:

"Whom do you represent?"

No reply. The other one was presumably going through my bag back there, but nobody searched me or even checked my passport. Then he came in and dumped the bag down on the floor. Then the three got up and followed him out. The train stopped. We all watched each other through the window for a few moments until the train started up again and they were gone. I sat back, a little dazed.

Eventually I was evicted from the compartment by a ticket inspector who didn't speak English. He was himself.

The cornered narrator *Lazare*, in the ruins of a world, mask-faced . . . The Chateau at La Roche woodland scene, attackers again dead of night "The full force of opposition." Stirring coffee listlessly disembodied conversation

I vomited the streets of Tangier *"Desire with loathing strangely mixed / On wild or hateful objects fixed"* the cop sitting crosslegged piles of carpets an American tourist flat on his back on the floor in the medina

"Heart attack" he said.

Eventually the majoun arrived money changed hands and we vamoosed out of there leaving him and his stiff post-haste.

It really hit the fan in Tangier. Inevitably. It's the place for it.

Lazare, in an old black plastic YSL raincoat, waiting, face gaunt, mask-like, Irish coffee on the table. "What does he now remember of Chateau Rouge?" The majoun was enough to give anyone heart failure. Terminal delirium, the images of the past decade in which he functioned, walked around and which enveloped him nightly "There are very few of us left . . ."

Rapid flashes out of body experiences — *DANGER! — LIVE RAIL!* — situation becoming increasingly hallucinated and menacing — The return ticket — (rapid flash back to train) — unnerving phone conversation with Bedaya — "I *have* to go —" The *Ka*, the parallel body, now the only area in which Bedaya can be contacted — "The only way to reach him is to follow him there. An extremely perilous procedure." Sink or swim. We never imagined how serious and dangerous things really were . . . we were taking enormous risks . . . and that of course was what had always frightened us —

"*No more extra time*" — Lost and suffering partial amnesia Bedaya deduces that he has been killed by Madame Ba, but cannot understand why. "He had been waylaid. That was a fact . . . he had to understand what to do about that." An old story.

Piecing the story together. The Two Boys, recognized as members of Bedaya's team — The Star again — "*We are from Home.*" Outside the bar Bedaya remembers that his old friend and adversary Madame Ba had insinuated Foutaise into his life in a devastating attempt to make him "love his enemy. As she did." Dark shadow hovering over Bedaya — eyes in a mirror dimming into blackness — Two lone figures on a deserted street as the sun goes down, blood-red . . . Vague fuzzy scene with the boys and a Third Man on the rue de Dunkerque. Scenery shifts into the office in Les Halles. The boys and the tax official.

Scene in the apartment with the boys. Bedaya described as "the weak centre of a weak circle."

Accusing manner of the boys, especially the younger of the two — glass front door, rue de l'Assomption — flickers intermittently — more accusations — the younger boy explodes — memories — *Vogue*, "the first member of our team that you really connected, here" — the school — Bedaya "using the Other Method to teach a 'true and different knowledge' . . ." The young boy's hysteria.

Into an abyss of Time . . . Rapid flashes of previous images and scenes — head falling — "the Other Method of another Time" — Madame Ba's strategy: blood-red. Fragmented memories of the Chateau training . . . "an alternative version of the history and manipulation of power . . ." rockclimbing — mist over the river — more discussion — Vogue — chicken scene with the young boy and Bedaya — room swirling around and around — Bedaya's voice, inaudible — momentary blackout — Vogue's voice, high in nowhere — Other angry voices cut in — "*Stop acting!"* the boy and the joint *"Remember the Chateau to be together!"*

"Grains of former mosaics . . ." Set up by Bedaya as a warring couple flash of Madame Ba an ageless angel of death her crystal ball and toilet "Journeys. Delirium "

"Let go! Let go!" The drug called *I Am Not Alone* "I am the senses and I am twisting" A small room, made of glass.

The effect of the drug . . . Sink or swim.

"For the limit, I am the one" said a spirit entity dedicated to inflicting the utmost stress and tension.

The reflective side of KJ shines forth in a telex he got through to the increasingly beleagured guests of the Grand Hotel Villa de France:

I could hardly focus . . .

GRANOTEL 33082APOSYNTHESIS . . .

AN OLIVE
WE GO WITH YOU TO SHADOW PATTERNS OF WORDWILL COMBINE AT LAST . . . MOUTH TO MOUTH . . . BREATHING UNION IN ELEGIES BY THE SNARL OF BUREAUCRATIC MUTABILITY. . .BLACK SUN SHADOWS CRESCENT MOON. . . THOUGHTS FLOW BARREN BONES DREAMS UNFOLD MIRACULOUS SECRETS LOVE IS PAINFUL AS LONELINESS. .. LISTEN . . . AN OLIVE LEAF FALLS GENTLY . . . FORGET MY PAIN NOW YOUR HELLENIC SOD IS BEFOULED. . . ORPHEUS . . . POLYPHONIC LYRE BEYOND WORD AND PEN AND SLEEP . . . GENTLY . .. SILVER LEAF IN SUNFILLED GLADE PERFECT HARMONY . . . YOU ARE OF PEOPLE . . . SOIL AND DREAM A SWEATING THIRSTY HEART . . . PERFECT SOUND IN PEACEFUL SHADE ANOINTED WOOD IN SURREAL DANCE BRANCH TO HEAVEN REACH AND TOIL STRESSES AND THEIR PAINS WAN MOONS ORTHODOX OLIVE YOU ARE NOT BYZANTINE SCHEMES. . . ENTWINED IN ANCIENT SOIL THE WORD THE IMAGE HALLOWED SAGA LIGHT DELIGHT AND SHELTERING WOMB PERFUMED TIME . . .

EARTH'S WARM HEAT PURIFYING SENSES SWIRL IN ANCIENT TRANCE . . . ORPHEUS EYES PALE WITH STRAIN YOU ARE . . . LIGHT AND LIFE...I ARION AND HASSAN BIN SABBAH CHUCKLE . . . PUT THE MUSIC TO THESE WORDS.
JKMC
BEST REGARDS
THE BOARD OF DIRECTORS
SUCCESS WITH YOUR PROJECT
RA ARRIVES FROM NEW YORK ON TUESDAY

"*Get back to the Ka*" advises some excruciating internal combustion fruit, eyes gleaming.

(*"These days, it's very low, broke my heart . . ."*)

(*"He's easily nice. That special relationship, that belief . . ."*)

"Can I borrow your match, old son?"

I handed them over.

It seems very cold and very early. Philippe, "the first member," had taken the train to Asilah to meet Larbi, Hamri's contact. I should have gone too. But here I have to meet these agents . . .

"When did you first meet the Green Man?" it sounded like he said.

Oh, the *Green* man.

"Yes, Mr Green . . . I met him in here, as a matter of fact . . . Some years back . . ."

(". . . I still want to see him, of course, that's my feeling. But it doesn't have that special *something* anymore. How could it? . . . I'm just trying to be as patient and tolerant as possible, to someone who's behaved so badly . . .")

It seems very cold and that's my feeling. The majoun was starting to take hold again.

Dreamy sequence in a car with Mr Green looking for La Roche — Brit. Intelligence flash of Kincora, Oldfield,etc — running for a train — a bus — scene on the bus with Bedaya and the Old Man — breakdown.

Tea with Mr Green and the duchess, conversation slowly more and more inaudible and dreamlike — ("Tomorrow . . . it doesn't — ")

"*It's only penicillin.*" — A book on croissants — ." "His legs were in the kitchen — "

Teeth marks.

Strained discussion with the two boys. Further discourse on Bedaya and his disputive team. Bedaya's "special knowledge". Street scene with the boy and the "enemy" a sickening shimmering horribly malevolent energy mass undersea tentacles whipping out of an old deeply corrupt core in all directions it recedes rapidly. The boy's face fades sun an arch of roses Bedaya at his table ". . . the unmistakable voice" "*All the fault of those* " sun french windows of the Chateau the stone garden an empty canvas trees shimmering dazzling flying Voice describing blurred and fuzzy flashes of street markets taxis "I'll remember you saying that" the two down below on the street shimmering dazzling consciousness flying Through a door night police at the door "*Ca va, ca va*" from the park bench is it the Old Man? graffiti-scratched staircase once ornate deafening noise from outside wind scattered ruins bells ringing as the attackers swarm forward a great white *flash*

Yes, I'd still like to see the fascinating Green Man . . . I had been away and after returning couldn't reach him. I phoned the Middlesex Hospital on impulse. He was there but leaving that afternoon so I went to collect him. He was barefoot. He showed me an ID card, mouth twisted into a kind of resigned snarl.

"No illusions" he said. I had always known him as Murray Smith.

I lost contact with Murray during the last period of travel with Jim. When I got back from our fateful meeting in Dusseldorf I learned that he had died. Heart attack.

"I wish I had a photo of him. There was one taken by . . . you know, Trolley Bus . . . ?"

"Oh, yes."

"I'd like to see that."

(*"Is not possible I talk to cops in Tunis . . ."*)

"I've been reading your book, *very* dangerous . . . *Just get away*." (Mr Green's voice)

Spidery barely legible handwriting dissolves into scenes from Mr Green's maliciously mocking alternative scenario . . . "*the compartments are moving forward . . . a porthole here and there . . . Is it a Whelme in his room in an empty unfurnished space station?"* Young man in the train compartment is seen to be Lazare before he was obliged or at least entitled to change his name — Whelme and Vogue on the train singing some kind of duet — *"We'll never forget what we'll never forget"* — They escape from the train disappearing into a vista of ruins — Dream voices from the bar —

"The morning ruined my name" — more ruins — a tacky stage set — They stand handcuffed together at the front of the stage singing the DPP song, Indignities.

(DPP allegedly stands for Displaced Person. Ominous KJ voiceover here growling *"Department of Public Prosecution".)*

Another vivid flash white plane rising in blackness — fog

"— only *one* of you! — "

A postcard: *No more extra time!* — Mr Green's mouth twists — wax dolls stuck through with pins — Hell Walk, an inferno of squirming Time — years of victory and devastation. Together in the dark looking back at the spectral ruins. The park bench: *on est tres mal ici.*

Ghosts in the bar talk about their "real names". Intelligence, magic and pure con inextricably entwined, as ever.

"Ours is the finkdom the power and the Story."

We flooded the hotel room in the midst of all this. There are only about four hours of running water in Tangier so you have to remember to turn off the taps but we were in no condition —

At seven in the morning the carpet from the corridor outside wrapped around the fountain in the courtyard to dry and KJ screaming down the line:

"WHATHERFUCKERYADOIN?!!"

It is the tension connected with the fear of what will happen and the shock when it does happen which are energizing. Or they can be. Of course it doesn't do to take this too far. You could get nervous.

We drove to Larache . . . Ira, Raphael, me, Philippe, Georges Bousquet, director of the Centre Culturel Francais de Tanger, his young assistant, plus the driver . . . unless it was the assistant who was driving, I don't remember . . . to visit Genet's grave or perhaps simply to get out of Tangier for awhile and pose for Ira over the remains . . . Perfect for Genet, the Spanish cemetery high on the clifftop flanked on one side by a bordello, on the other by a prison, the great Phoenician harbour of Larache at his feet . . .

Re-entry problems   drowned in sensation   "*Stay up!*"   pulled out from under   "Are you inside me?" Stomping feet. The waterfront hotel and the key   the wireless   "OUT of here!" The apartment, voices, dark glasses. Trying to make some notes about the drug, IANA, but hard to focus . . . you are lying on a mat . . . a few embers left among the stones and the leaves of Bedaya . . . your body lies in darkness, heavy as mine . . . The Man From Nowhere, invisible, incorporeal, seeing but not seen . . . far away

. . . a disembodied eye . . .

A note dropped onto the table. A sinister trio. "You poor *thing*!"

KJ phone conversations   he has been reported as under arrest in Spain after billion dollar dope bust. Cops confirm and then deny. "Better the Welsh rarebit than the Fox."

(When the pioneering Welsh-born cannabis entrepreneur Howard Marks was arrested on Ibiza in 1988 all the British papers announced that KJ had been nabbed along with him: IRA (sic) MAN ARRESTED IN SPAIN   in The Times, 26 July, he was the only person actually named. In fact, it is said, Marks had been arrested along with his wife and two colleagues, a Mr Kenion, and William R. Reaves, known for his past services to the Medellin Cartel, the Central Intelligence Agency and other such savoury organizations. KJ's name was substituted for that of Reaves, who in due course found it expedient to put the finger on Jim when the famous Fox finally did get his tail wet, publicity conspicuous by its total absence, Germany, 1991.)

Facility: "I really *must* contact KJ . . ." Lazare staring fixedly at the mouthpiece of the phone before putting it down   Flash back to bar jukebox: "*She got a floating bracelet, green eyes and gabby breath . . .*"

Smoking . . ."Do you have *any* idea what it is, the brain?" . . . stirring coffee listlessly . . . atmosphere resonant of first meeting with his contact, but he is alone.

The flickering room, breathing mosaics with Bedaya and the Old Man — the Old Man's finger — "Remember THAT?" — The psychic phantasmagoria, a cosmic Disneyland of mock horror . . . awe-inspiring but somewhat tiresome — total impossibility — the mirrors — Suspension in space the whole city spread out below — A vertiginous landing-strip, coming toward us . . .

Moss, leaves, vines, clinging to crumbled grandeur — sun on the leaves — Lazare, lost, delirious, yammering like a demented desert nabi — "Flooded is my name!" — The sun goes down, a single star irradiating the scene, a country scene with Bedaya, briefly located. Walking back to the house. Sudden ominous halflight, snow, phone chirruping like an angry bird — angry conversation — Other voice sounds to be that of Vogue — *"Say something different!"* With the two boys. The young boy's taunts — the boys fight — " — *you ain't seen nothing YET!"* The mirror — a burning red glow around the face — Bedaya's face superimposed — Menacing bobs of light dance on the street — The Old Man in the basement cafe.

Cop scene with the young boy and Mr Green — Gunfire — window explodes in Paris.

KJ under duress throws a press conference — *"They're trynah deprive me of my chivil libertiesh!"* — KJ trailing diplomatic plates, codenames, false passports, dummy corporations, etc, etc, harangues cowed audience — *"The allegations are serious lies! I admit nothing attack the evidence remake myself and survive! — From the Belfast ghetto —"* — a car exhaust explodes from outside and everyone hits the floor. KJ is already out the door. Back at his fortified French residence he is down on his knees rummaging through bones and ashes from the incinerator . . . the duchess has demanded Bedaya's ashes . .. "Ah, last night's chicken, sure it is . . ." He scoops them up into an urn.

KJ, in the can for a good part of two years now and no great desire to let him out in the near future, if ever. Twenty-three hours a day solitary. High security, like living in a steel bubble. The charge being conspiracy of course. Conspiracy to do exactly what, they are still investigating. Presumably they have a cornucopia of choice, KJ has been conspiring since the day he was born, in whatever disputed year that was. Everything is disputed about KJ.

"The Fox . . . international playboy from the mean streets of Belfast" . . . "conman" . . . (KJ has perpetrated more on the Blarney Stone than merely kissing it) . . . "revolutionary guru" . . . "cultural incendiarist" . . "How many times have his most apparently maniacal assertions and accusations been proven entirely accurate?" Ask me another.

I first met Jim around 1985, a year or so before Brion died. I had known of his existence for some time but had no real idea of who he actually was, like most people to this day. He was James Kennedy at the time. After knowing and liking him for a few years I once had the temerity to ask: "But what *is* your game, really?"

"Can you repeat what you said?"

I did.

"But you don't understand, I'm a Jesuit, really" he replied.

He kept Brion alive for the last few years and took nothing back. And he did much the same for me thereafter. And others too. Handy Dandy indeed. "You're into things with him and then you don't know what you are into" I remember Ramuntcho Matta saying, retreating from a bar in Paris. Rumour and any amount of malicious misinformation ran rife "Kennedy" had power over Brion, he had "no credibility" at all, his real name was McCann, a celebrated arms/dope/you-name-it dealer who was about to take everything.

"*Destroy this letter immediately!*" wrote Facility with her big red heavy pen.

I took it to Brion immediately. I was disturbed, I knew he was weakened and in danger from those increasingly around him. I didn't keep a copy. He read it, frowned and threw it into the garbage. Jim arrived very soon and we spoke for the first time. He gave me a good deal of money and asked me to stick around. Now, more than ever, I didn't know whether or not these bloodsuckers gathering around Brion were really in his employ

(KJ of course treats practically everyone as an employee, he owns the place where he happens to be.) But Jim took nothing, except the *Makemono*, to which he was well entitled. It would never have been executed without the energy of his persuasion.

Was it a month we spent in Tangier, of which I can remember practically nothing, and still less of that which followed   Flash of more team conflict back at the apartment — The Psychic Ten headquarters, Ile St Louis — Lazare, tracking Bedaya through the wastes — terrible winds — flowers fly past — his head drops — "Stay up!" — images from the IANA drug experiences — "the senses and I are twisting — I'm going back with him — no more extra time —"

Sorcerers strew traps and pitfalls all about them, as Brion said . . . sometimes so frantically they fall flat on their faces into one themselves, as he might have said. KJ must of course forever be a prime example of this and my approach to his interminable Harry Lime routine is almost entirely contra the popular official manic criminal-terrorist-con artist version: That of a certainly somewhat manic cultural heretic. (As Brion also said, a magician must be outside the Law, outside the domain of Law and therefore not regulated by it. "He is in constant danger not only from the orthodox community but from himself, due to the derangement of the senses which his products provide . . .") A trickster savant, certainly the most spectacularly impressive I have come across. KJ of course delights in terrorizing — sometimes anybody he can get his hands on, it seems — with perfect aplomb he phones total strangers spitting commands — sometimes governments if you listen to him, and I can believe it, just about.

For my part, I found him overwhelmingly authoritative, profound, silly, cruel, malicious, threatening, kind, but most particularly — as with other teachers I have met — funny. For the most part, even in the most extreme situations (no shortage of those with KJ), his behaviour and conversation — more or less the same thing — convulsed me with delight.

Well . . . throw him a fish . . .

Flooded temples . . . with Bedaya and the Old Man . . . "A fullblown flooded saint . . ." Bedaya choking with laughter . . . they both fade, an odd spectral light suffuses the room. The window. The Star. The apartment in dissaray. Construction workers . . . high spralling clouds . . .

"*Doctor T! — Thousand Fingers!*" — Vogue's voice — manic parody of Lazare's overblown delirium — (Arab market scenes cut in here) — desperate hilarity — "Hope to hear from you soon" —

Scene with the boys and the soup. They fall asleep. People walking in every direction "*Are you coming?*" (they have all lost their shoes)

Facility and Mr Green walking in a dark ominous street Mr Green seen to be barefoot "Are you coming?" palpable menace in these scenes (it is obvious that Mr Green is going to get the spike) Howling dogs Bedaya closer and closer more and more solid

He sits back from the typewriter gaze fixed frozen, The Star, candles, ruined staircases of the Chateau, a spectral bridge with many crossing explosion walls and staircases collapsing

"*Where are we now ?*" Facility and Mr Green. "We're near the rue de l'Offensif."

"*Where?*"

The spectral rue de l'Offensif swaying passage through to the apartment a canvas coming alive NO MORE EXTRA TIME!

A great glass door explodes french windows crash to smithereens a blinding flash The young boy walking hurriedly for the train dodging cops through the Arab market turns abruptly is struck by a crushing force and wakes in the arms of the other

"Are you *coming*?"

Past flashes of Mr Green, the cafe in Pigalle "Like it was designed by Ba" his mouth quivers into a thin grimace as he consults an oracle, staring deeply, The Star hovers . . .

"*We're going back?*"

"*Yes, it's over . . .*" The two boys.

Facility and Mr Green approaching a streetlight . . . rue de l'Assomption . . . (Strains of the DPP song)

"*You're so lucky! Really, Murray, you'll have such a comfortable death!*"

Clouds in a blue sky forming Mr Green . . . cane, raincoat over an arm, suit, tie . . . floating in the sky . . ."*Au revoir,* Mr Green"

. . . Mr Green staring down from the sky . . . He drifts languidly, over . . .

Three figures in hotel room Bedaya, Lazare, Vogue Bedaya is trying to make some notes about the drug, Vogue is lying on a mat at the side of the bed.

Vogue, Lazare and the telephone. (Lazare slams it down.) Sleep.

Bedaya and Lazare (Vogue still asleep):

"Are you ready to work for me again?"

"Whenever wasn't I?"

"In about ten minutes . . . ?"

Voice fading — silence — hoarse crackling — "So much opposition" — KJ's voice cut in with Lazare's —

KJ: "Continue by means of the Third, call when it becomes necessary —"

"You know we intend to —"

Two glasses of Irish coffee clink together, the beginning of a new age.

Then the accidents started — (and, as we know from our training, there ain't any such animal) — Paris-Barcelona — train stopped by car crash — (KJ is already unavoidably detained) — when we got there the French boy and the two Italians — blood and glass in all directions — they survived — we were already getting the hell out of there the Puerto Rican pimp the two fags and the midget, and Jacky the dancing boy drew the heat for the *second* time last night a DJ saved his life — too bad — I am planning to off them all however many broken bones it takes — *"SECURITY RISKS!"* KJ screams, as he picks up and incorporates more and more and more of these jerks into his international vaudeville act the Baron launches off the balcony here at the Twins' in Cadaques breaking just about everything — *"Did you get the key?"* asks Carlos a few hours before *his* gallery goes up in smoke and all of Dali's leftover lemmings are screaming bloody murder slapping each other around and the inevitable cops and ambulance — well, we got out of there too. Stuart the enigmatic Mr Old Days is on hand to get us back across the border and his tyre miraculously blows at Perpignan on the dusty track to a military police establishment. We finally made it to the station.

So, we are more or less in freak-out territory, to put it mildly . . . in Professor Wasserstein's words, "a world of such bizarre and complex conspiratorial activity that it seemed impossible to disentangle truth from rumour, propaganda stunts or psychological warfare, let alone downright lies —"

"DON'T PANIC!"

"*Jim* "

"You're *fuckin panicking!* wha ? And fuck you too! "

"*Wha* ?"

"No it's this stupid bitch here Yeah, *fuck you!* "

"Uh, Jim "

"*Call you back* "

I slammed the phone down, spraying red paint in all directions Old days, altogether changed Graffiti on Brion's door Dawn. A monstrous wind whips the Caves of Hercules, outside Tangier. Facility and a menage of hangers-on Foutaise, etc have assembled to conduct the Rites of Pan tossing the ashes over the sea the wind whips them back into their faces Young boy screaming: "*If HE were coming, you would see the flipping light of Heaven's dick!*" chicken sound effects

Fire from KJ's incinerator superimposed over Makemono as Djebala trance music works to a crescendo.

Last mountains God knows where. The original inhabitants of this supposedly sacred area and everyone else disappeared.

Violence is red roses and shoes the stars are beginning to fall . . .

"WHAT are your intentions?"

(A policeman typing our answers)

"To underline, and therefore reinforce, the nobility of the human spirit and its deepest intention: to transcend all its awful attendant traumas to the extent that the spirit may no longer be human" Space here for assorted KJ outrages rummaging through bones and ashes from the incinerator "Ah, *Lazare, Vogue, Bedaya, KJ,* sure it is . . ." He scoops them up into an urn . . .

An article on "Mad *Ka*'s Disease" in the *Daily Lama* . . . "Perhaps ultimately the most significant point is their final and total failure. They did not overthrow the existing order; they did not even succeed in holding a single city of any size . . ."

Indeed . . . "That which failed but which is still going on."

(Bedaya.)

We do not expect *success* in this area. (Achievement, yes.) Why did Operation Trance fail? Because of the delusion of succeeding *here*.

Fire from KJ's incinerator — new tools of attack —

"WHAT ARE YOU DOING? — Hate-practitioner of the Nervous System! Terrorist! — You cannot *rewrite* or blackmail history work at the receiving and transmitting centre — !"

Poison and fear . . . in the course of so many cities . . . of any size . . . of delusion — of succeeding *here* — Dusseldorf to Amsterdam — Tangier — "DON'T PANIC BROTHER!" — Berlin — "We have no pity, we have guns and we *NO — N-O* — the cop's attitude!" — trying not to scream often with laughter at the same time

"GEMME A FUCKIN DRINK!"

Backtracking, sidetripping — *"Cool, DISCREET! — GARCON! — UNDER CONTROL! — I'VE PLANNED EVERYTH — "*

Maniacal indiscretion in a bar. All the way back to Germany. The flaw was his.

CHANGING THE CUT-OUTS

(The Living Dead)

Hugely-drunken theatrical-type lunatic lurches through the door profusely sweating braying Olivier-like: *"Beware my follower!"*

He reels over to the bar "Sweet burning *enfer! a drink!"* -and turns back to his dim audience. The last all drink.

"The Shadow tracks thy flight of fire *night is coming!* all smothered up in shade does sit Glamorous Granny, macabre proliferating species to creep forth again!"

Jesus, I mumbled, this just about is the limit, and got up to go.

He glares at me or who or whatever he is seeing, maniacally:

"For this, I'll never follow thy pallid fortunes more. Who seeks and will not take, when once 'tis offered, shall never find it *more!*"

"Smoked transcendence is accessible to all" I said, echoing Brion. Or so one might like to think.

So maybe I better stop trying to sell you another novel and finally tell you what the whole scene really is . . .

Well, I was leafing through some old press clippings just sent from Paris, and there he was, Bedaya, Massa Brahim in full flow: "Poor Brion" lamenting his lack of success, beyond disappointment! "I guess I'm just hopeless!" Hah! The last time I heard from him he said I think for the second or who knows how many times, us donkeys are so dumb that he could be heard but is too drunk to come out and be seen, at least as I can understand it. We can talk. And then a real old familiar shuddering as Massa Brahim John C.B.L. Gysin, von Liestal, in full flow, swept my body . . .

I am some old clippings from Paris and there I talk . . .

And all I can think – it's catching – is what the sweet burning hell of a Massa Brahim von Liestal *et cetera-etc* situation have I got into and how, on earth, can I get out of it? as I remember from years back:

"You don't know what it is you are trying to get into."

Who does? Into or out of, really? That's how Masters get around and stay around. Or so one might hope. I guess I'm just hopeless.

He laughed, as only he could, genuine, kind amusement, really himself.

("Yes . . . but the *scene*, really is . . . ?)

Yes . . . *coming!* – *More!* Brion. *Access!* Stay around, shudder one night through the shadow tracks Massa Bedaya Brahim Gysin von-You-don't-know-who.

"Night is hopeless" he said.

Okay, so I guess I'm just a situation he seeks and will get out of *Smoked burning enfer!* – I understand it!

(Duck everyone, this could go anywhere.)

Call from AB 9.30 AM discarnate. Says he is speaking through a voice distorter and cannot say where he is. He seems to think my memoirs, which he is filming. "A deep-cover operation to infiltrate an ancient revolutionary movement." Advises me to alternate drinking hot and cold water. And "Stay away from the Kennedys."

("He couldn't put the life on the right rivers . . . and he was through." BG)

And all, life and death, is all mysteriously left.

The activities of the onetime-sometimes-beneficent can-go-anywhere foundation – itself somewhat discarnate (after getting out of the slammer) – have, following a plethora of ludicrously malicious communication of late been restricted to harbouring notorious American Zionist shoplifters and psuedo Islamic-anarchist affiliates of the Abu Nuwas Society for the Study of Sexual Culture in the Middle East (or any other direction presumably), a dimwitted Dublin initiate of which recently tried to sell Marianne Faithfull a binbag of T-shirts they are big into T-shirts for £50. Feet of clay, clear up to the neck.

I am emphasising the climate changes during this last glacial age.

After Brion's death some eyebrows were raised when, invited to contribute to Gladys Fabre's catalogue which would accompany a retrospective at the Galerie de France in Paris, I quoted Brion as saying that "People are shit" and asserted that despite all his relentless protestations to the contrary, Brion was neither neglected nor unsuccessful. "He simply had extremely powerful enemies."

He had made his mark, passed on his *"strong black"* to Burroughs (he had said that he could see that Burroughs was possessed by such a corrosive spirit that only such a radical method could possibly accomodate it) and whipped up a cosmic storm. With meagre financial recompense, naturally. *They* stood back, finally, let him become a Chevalier of arts and letters, get photographed with successful showbiz personalities and generally be befriended by assholes of the universe. As he said, they are shit.

He of course never achieved either the recognition or wealth accumulated by a Warhol, if that was what he wanted, needed, desired and I suppose it was. Presumably he died richer than Rimbaud, if that makes up for it.

The main infiltration/obstruction directed towards this certainly somewhat elderly movement was concerned with *preventing further development.*

And who is it who (not for the first time) actually tried to infiltrate a venerable revolutionary movement? one green card after another? -

Why, not our everloving con KJ, surely?

And could this ancient system really have been taken in by same? Well, *yesss* if necessary and *No*, not at all!

We of course always welcome wealthy Time, that which ends.

When I would ask Brion about the "actual techniques taught or used there" (Alamut) or broached other suchlike slippery area, he would clam up. He didn't know. He was just a sorcerer's apprentice. Now, I feel much the same. In Dublin, at the Here To Go show, 1992, there was a public session called "Remembering Brion" where some of the usual suspects were assembled to drag out the usual stuff – ("*Brion*, who invented the Dreamachine, *Brion*, who turned to me in the bus after the light flickering between the trees had spaced him out and said: '*Wow*! Man, like you're the Prophet of the Beat! I swear to Allah that if this thing gets off the ground I'll cut you in for half the bucks!' but being a man of integrity I -" *CUT!*) –

I for my part answered that, for me, this was extremely difficult because (where is everybody?) I simply did not *remember* Brion in the usual sense. To do so to *really* remember him requires an enormous effort of recapitulation because what he taught was not accessible to ordinary consciousness. The only way to reach him is to follow him there. What on earth really happened to me? What techniques? Where is everybody? Don't know.

"*Worn-out pals of dust, I ride with you, though I walk through the mess, into the grave softly carefully for his name's sake . . .*"

Whelme was an experienced agent, known as Lazare as required in the trade

"*We offer Space and one of the hundred sellers, even though seen before, comes strolling in, old on the principle myself. Attributable to one or two things, the pickup not so fast as it would be with the kind of person you think is correct . . .*" – *an enormous effort.*

As far as KJ was concerned, he came in *late*, and with a vengeance. And we followed him there into a dangerous, hilarious, coked-up vulgarian existence reeling from one nonsensically scandalous scam after another, forever on the road This is Lazare from here, there, nowhere, essentially

One man's mania. That was in several other countries and the deal is dead.

Gone, with the missing library and the Space Account. Once thought no longer

Today, all the roaring camps are gone, the thought waves towns, highways, countryside, mountain and desert . . . A few hours later, cities, lonely under the sky . . .

Lowered asbestos suspenders looked over our shoulders and there, finished, faded, never stop . . . *Appointment.*

THE DARKNESS CURSE

(Playing For Time)

"Integrity: Alone, at work, in secret . . . your story is Human Time, floor to floor, it dwindles, and darkness until the top if need be. Your life is nobody else's fidelity to his curse."

Mr Green's Oracle

"This is Jacket from Eleven Plus. A tough school."

"Fine times."

"Sit down, Jacket."

"Now, with regard to the missing library and the Space Account. We do meet these problems and have met them previously. These are intervals, difficulties which affect the small past . . ."

"Your story is Human Time, School."

"Thank you, I suppose."

I feel like someone who has been beamed down in a test tube, through which I can penetrate only occasionally as my hands glide through the glass reaching out to a dream typewiter . . . But not all that easy. Memory, as I say, is not up to it. I was mediator for a process that is dead. It's a plot, but not as we know it . . .

And I steer clear of medical subjects. Too much to say. Neurotics who run for a specialist at the drop of a cat don't like to hear it.

(Five AM. "Well, I'm really sorry to hear about Lucky." Jesus. Not that I didn't like Lucky . . . hit by a truck it seems . . . Just took me awhile to remember who he was. "I hope Butch and Sundance are okay?" Why not Leopold and Loeb?)

One moment they're walking around with "I've got a dumptruck in my balls" all over their T-shirts, before too long it will inevitably have reached the brain.

Captain C.T. Arbuthnot, CDM, DFN, God knows what, Retd., late of Her Majesty's whoever: *My Battle Against Athlete's Foot (Vol. I)*. Privately published, not surprisingly, 1929. A hefty and hilarious tome volume II of which has been denied us. Perhaps the captain had succumbed to his fungoid Nemesis or advanced dementia in the meantime.*

(An alleged volume of Captain Arbuthnott's table talk, also unsurprisingly, turned out to be non-existent. Presumably the guests would have been chained to the table. Old Stringer Marchbanks of the Poona Horse lurches to his feet — "I'm buggered if I can stand any more of this!"

They work away with files and hatchets while the captain yaps on oblivious, bare foot up on table.)

His last words are said to have been: "*Courage, Mary*," apropos nothing in particular.

Sir Francis Younghusband, *etc, etc* — taking time off from the Great Game accompanied by his faithful pony-man Mahmood — was photographed at the graveside in thoughtful mood, head high pondering the Realms . . .

But things have been looking up on the Arbuthnott front. His monumental *Battle* — subtitled: *A Victory* — is to be republished complete and unexpurgated (Paris: Pevaryl Press) and I am awaiting an advance on the old nut's biography. Sponsors: The National Blood Agency.

At least that is what the said Blood Agency likes or pretends to think I'm working on. From my point of view, I know as much about Captain Arbuthnott and his condition — what it is to see egomania boil to its limit, burn at the stake — as I ever want to, bread or no bread.

Probably, no teacher has ever spoken to you like this before.

But perhaps this is cloud-work, for when the delirium is at its height

* Arbuthnott had a point. He was fascinated by the raison d'etre of this unwanted lodger.

the clouds often return and join the late of Her Majesty's . . . whatever . . We both know we are talking nonsense.

Nobody *I* know keeps switching the programme control –

(Standing outside a cinema – *"Queen of the Nile"* starring Mrs Dwelley)

Facility close. The intrepidness of The Wind. The outstanding aspect of her personality soldiered on with a vengeance – "meet these problems and have met them previously" – Playing for Time. Imperial brightness of the Masonry.

(– *"Surely everyone must have by now"* Philip West, fourteen years old. The flipping light of Heaven's dick. School Time, barely audible. Playfellows in the rude palaestae. The small past.)

"But that was not the original – *God knows,* the original intention – what was it? It wasn't that."

Bedaya, attempting not only to defy fate, but to rule it.

"They did not, fully."

The Process is a Combination-Time, nearly wrecked the planet.

"Is this really wise?"

The show is falling, no doubt. A tough floor-to-floor, the Darkness curse. The delirium at its height, there, sit down, Jacket.

Buchan's *The Power House* occupied our thoughts a lot at one period . . .

"'I tell you the division is a thread, a sheet of glass. A touch here, a push there, and you bring back the reign of Saturn' . . ."

Burroughs, throwing his chop-finger up in front of my face:

"Remember *that*?"

Scene from *The Thirty-Nine Steps* . . . What a scene . . . rue St Martin, Paris, early eighties, I could hardly see through the smoke . . .

I'm doing my best.

"Courage, Mary."

Last words as I say of the Good Captain A – not his real name anyway. Also known as . . . Green Gables, was it?

("In this game you must drop the curtain neat and pat at the end of each scene, if you don't want trouble later with the missing heir and the family lawyer.")

Well Jacket it is a Great Game and you are the man for it, no doubt.

"Whatya got in mind, a Nike advertisement?"

Huuum. I ordered another pellagra.

I knew what Arbuthnott remembered . . . the bent old men, the dank picturesque hovels . . . he was best man in his best scarlet and black. Despite his girlish eyes, Sandy had courage, real courage, and Mary would need it too. Bucketsful. Old Sandy . . .

Mud on his black boots, all these knowing old crones and cowed, respectful brats they were in their bloody place in those days escorting them through the Victorian hilltop village of the 90s. Dear, blushing Mary would love and need it too. Sandy . . . ? Well . . . Never happier than when parading through the Empire dressed up to the nines . . . (Even Francis didn't know if it was Mahmood or Sandy half the time . . .)

"In the very front, now nearing the city rampart . . . one man . . . driven, like the point of a spear soon to be driven home, turbaned like one possessed . . . As he rode it seemed like the fleeing Turks sank by the roadside with eyes strained after his unheeding figure . ." This was in Wiltshire.

"Give me a break."

Got up from head to foot in Tuareg drag face uplifted, arms outstretched like wings, pulling the moon behind him in a net, he was never any good in England. They were always sending him out to the Hindu Kush or somewhere, anywhere as far away as possible.

(Singing:) *Sandy the Great, Sandy the Wise, teller of truth, hater of lies, laughed as he fought, till the men died . . . and on and on until we meet the journey's end . . .*

(Edward Said is quoting Victor Hugo somewhere around here)

"I am a British officer on special assignment and can say no more" he informed the magistrate imperiously. He never went out again after that . . . didn't have much choice.

"And the poor, bent old Mary the hilltop village remembered."

Jacket, looking as if he might easily scream, hastily orders a drink.

Well . . . be that as it may . . . As I say this is just the job for you J and we must proceed, regardless of the fearful outlook . . .

The Donner Party limps onward . . . Survivors of he Forlorn Hope.

"Let's hope the weather holds."

The Indian said he could not find the road. He wrapped a blanket around himself and stood under a tree all night.

"Never take no cut-offs and hurry along as fast as you can" I muttered to myself.

(In 1846 the hapless Donner Party – trying the "fast route" from Illinois to California – after an already nightmare haul across the Great Salt Lake finally made it to the Sierra Nevadas and came to a frozen standstill. Eventually some of the stronger members calling themselves *The Forlorn Hope* split from the others and attempted to continue the treck through the mountains. Treachery, murder and eventually and most notoriously cannibalism ran rampant through both parties. One unrepentant survivor later put his experience to good avail and opened a restaurant.)

"Can't you get this turbaned tosser to *move*?"

I was wrapped in my tweeds. J was shivering.

"He's waiting for the light, apparently."

Dawn again. Overcast, the morning lowers, and heavily in clouds brings on the day . . ."A little light and a little water brought him out of his DAZE." I was reading *The Mystery of Edwin Drood*:

"And if I do not clearly express what I mean . . . it is either for the reason that having no conversational powers, I cannot express what I mean, or that having no meaning, I do not mean what I fail to express. Which to the best of my belief, is not the case."

An unaccountable expedition indeed. Some dung-cakes built a fire. The hookah glowing red on the brass tweezers. Even now the darkness.

And we tottered on, both rather ill at ease, across these most un-Moorish of moors at the fakir's dictate.

J could contain himself no longer.

"For Christ's sake, this is Bodmin Moor, not Peshawar – !"

Eddies of mist swirled around. Mahmood hovered in the distance.

"We're faced with a band of unstable states stretching from the Caucasus to Cornwall, O chela."

J frowned. "Bands of rain more likely."

Later much later, it was dark, black. A spectral victorian pile finally loomed into sight. The Indian had vanished into the mist.

"Bleak House, I presume."

J is coming on like the wiseacre crime reporter in a 1940s haunted house movie.

"I bet the servant's a character."

We approached and I rapped loudly at the door.

A horrible wracking emphysematic cough heralded the arrival and the entrance grated open to reveal a wraithlike apparition got up in antique shawls, mufflers, at least two ratty overcoats from head to toe.

"Hello, Doome."

"Sod the chest" it croaked and let us in.

J's bravado appeared momentarily to have deserted him.

"Doom" he muttered, still standing in the doorway.

"With an e."

"Jesus."

We followed the bent shuffling form through the hall into the dank, dimly-lit dining room and settled ourselves while Doome creaked around in the darkness. There was red wine, and some mature cheese.

"Our host?" I yelled abruptly, startling J. Doome was somewhat deaf. When he wanted.

"You'll be wanting to see the potting shed."

"Kind!" I yelled again.

"An it's the annual cleaning of the rafters tomorrow."

I slammed the glass down onto the table and rose stiffly, glaring at him.

"I do not know, and even knowing . . . 'E turns up in a long arriving ."

I sat down.

"There are souls musbe saved and souls musnot be saved" he announced and disappeared into an alcove, much to J's apparent relief.

We retired, exhausted, Doome's death rattle leading the way.

Forgotten cupboards, dusty attics . . .

"You're going to miss me" Bedaya said.

I said something to the effect that I'd been missing him for quite some time. He took the point.

Impossible to describe the elation of being in his presence once more — no question that it was post-death. He was referring to yet another perhaps "definitive" separation. Brave, brave man, don't ever stay away from me, now I am just a brave brave man like you. Big big man —

"The waggapaggabagga is full tonight" — Bedaya-speak for wastepaper basket — cream from Menton, toothpaste from Eastleigh, newspapers, "The Beast of Bodmin" -

Thoroughly dissociated — *"Doom"* I uttered involuntarily — *"DOOM!"* J echoed — my own voice into another door grated open — to reveal a maniacal manifestation: *Doome!* — was it? — naked except for a sequinned bra and helmet face contorted into a samurai grimace ranting dementedly — inexpressible horror — the outermost threshold — a great wailing

"Umbrae! — shadows in my way! — uninvited guests! — Wars! — hostility from all! — worse than civil! — And sanction granted to wrong! — Turn conquering swords! — there are the powerful! — bloodied in their own hearts! — Embattled kin-ranks! — Guilt shared by all! — And standards set against enemy standards! — Then Discord's orders were fulfilled on earth! — Matched eagles! Threatening javelins! — Judgement in the Sunday Room! — The Eternal House!"

The dead of night drops javelins sheerly down.

Quite useless. Rubbing an analgesic cream onto my shoulder, staring out at the dismal misty scene, vast, barren, desolate, shivering.

"Not a living soul" I murmured.

J came ambling in from the bathroom.

"Turned out nice again."

The cough announced the approach and the door creaked slowly open.

"Hullo, darling" said J jauntily.

Doome shot him a withering glare and put down the breakfast tray.

"Doome!" I muttered, wincing involuntarily.

"DOOME!" J echoed. "With an e. I was forgetting."

"Darling's the local shepherd. He blows the bellows . . ." I mumbled, my head swimming slightly. J stared. "For the church organ."

"I should have known."

"An the Lord is biggern both of us:" croaked Doome and tottered off, like an old ram with the footrot.

"Onto state affairs."

J was sitting on the bed.

"So, you know Doome."

"He's been around since the silent days."

"And you've been here before."

I nodded.

"So why did we have to get dragged 20 or 30 miles across a Cornish bog by some character dressed as a fucking Indian? The is a road around here presumably."

"Those were the instructions."

"Who from?"

". . . Signed: *The Superiority Complex*."

"And who might they be, if I dare ask?" J's frown was becoming permanent.

"They may be an affiliate of the National Blood Agency, from whom I have been receiving money for no discernible reason."

"They sound like they could go well tegether" J sighed. "And *Kind*?"

"A Dutchman, who looks like a Greek. Or a Greek who says he's a Dutchman, I don't know. He's been missing for quite some time."

"Maybe he's in the potting shed."

Increasingly somewhat befuddled . . . pitch black lanes of Commonmoor, branches hung over with eternal drizzling rain into the rushing river, rough stone walls and eerie gorse-covered mire . . . this is mid-afternoon . . . the story obscures everything, a rickety footbridge over fantasy, vanishing Cornwall squelching under my Tricker Trackers. The landlord of the jocularly-named *Keep Out*, a huge weather-beaten man (“What's *his* name, Parsnip or something?” J put in) was holding the fort and holding forth on the Beast of Bodmin. The local folklore department.

"Its eyes are great yellow orbs. An it as a foul scream like a woman's but hundred times magnified -"

("Courtesy of the National Sound Archive, I assume.")

"There'll be no rabbits or foxes about and the birds at Jamaica Inn stop singing. That's the call for caution made by Daphne du Maurier . . . 'You mustn't bend over or run' . . ."

"Broken neck stomach ripped open from sternum to leg."

"Many have met their deserts so . . ."

("A cat goes in, kills and eats. Very little mess. Animal wars.")

Having presumably missed out on the annual rafter ablutions, we trudged back to the house under the dull hard sky. We crossed the actual Darling on the way.

"Silly old people" he slurred blearily, staggering onwards through oozy fens, knee-deep drains.

J went inside. I had definitely decided to case the potting shed.

"Happy is he who can know the causes of things" I murmured to myself, dragging open the Iron Age door. "Who treads underfoot all fear, inexorable fate and vain rumour " – took half a step and experienced a sharp intake of breath. There was no floor. And from the pitch blackness of the abyss there wafted an indescribably sweet, nauseating, suffocatingly odorous vapour, like wine? milk? honey? – *etcetera*? I had no torch and not much desire to see or smell more. I wasn't about to dirty my Burberry. I stepped back and closed the door on this somewhat unpleasant portal.

"The principal of life" I muttered.

"I checked out the potting shed."

"Fascinating, I daresay."

I told him about it.

"So, the potting shed, not surprisingly, stinks. What do you deduce from that?"

"The potting shed is a *tomb*. A vertical pit going down, I imagine, into a cellar with an arched roof, into which is poured various fluids, most particularly blood."

"With any particular purpose in mind?"

"The seat of life. Reanimation of and communication with spirits."

"So where do they get blood?"

"Immolation of the local livestock. Known as omophagy. Seems to be the local scene . . . Presumably the farmers are insured . ."

"So now we're getting around to where Doome is actually centuries old and keeping himself alive — if that's the word — by unnatural means. I mean, this Cold Comfort Farm routine . . . I don't buy it.

I didn't blame him.

"I'm surprised you ever heard of Cold Comfort Farm. Your training didn't take in Franz Cumont?* He was taught when I was here."

It was one of the Centres . . . Doone was pretty much the same. It certainly seems like centuries. Obviously I don't remember much . . . What it had become in the meantime don't ask me . . . The Mysteries of Mithra, apparently . . . **

"Silly old people."

I pushed open a creaky farm gate with warning attached:

WILD BIG CATS
- KEEP OUT

descending into a public subway to my left newspaper hoarding POLICE RAID DOOM CULT — loud crashes — screaming wailing shouting — I jerked up in bed with a start, awake and shaking.

All quiet. J in the adjoining room had apparently heard nothing. I decided to check, got up, slipped on my djellaba and went to the stairs, half terrified at the thought of finding Doome in full regalia.

A shaft of light in the hall was illuminating the surface of a small writing desk. A notepad and pencil. I drifted down.

The top sheet of the pad bore the imprint of heavy handwriting. Well ....why not? I picked up the all too handy pencil and started to trace

smokes hashish and immerses himself in history.
He is obviously good, obviously insane. Is this
really wise?

Hmmm . . . my "very own words."

* Belgian author of *After Life in Roman Paganism* and *Oriental Religions in Roman Paganism*, etc.

** Another Cumont title. A study of the Persian Mysteries. The Mithraic culture almost succeeded in topping the Christian in the race for ideological dominance of pagan Rome.

I tore off the sheet, took the pencil again and wrote

NO

heavily on the next, then tore that off too. Replacing the pencil neatly by the pad I climbed grimly back to the bedroom.

I didn't think What is going on here? As far as I was concerned the plot here was to scare J witless, as part of his J training. The old cathartic rites, wise or otherwise. I was his overseer. It seemed the tables had been turned. It wasn't necessary to believe J had actually written the note. But someone had. And how had he slept through such a cacophany?

A pencil and notepad, really . . . what next? Rolling a joint at 3 AM I felt old and tired. Although my night was not yet over, I had decided to say nothing.

What little I had learned was certainly in harmony with previous engagements. Nothing so wearing as dodging assassins. If you're strong, you survive, but what it has cost you, the strength they have taken from you . . .

Well, often our stalkers went this way in the gay pursuit of a perilous quest.

I turned off the light and was just about settling in comfortably ten minutes later when: BANG: *crash*: banshee wails, howling, all the rest of it started up again.

"Quite a nap" I mumbled, lurched out of bed threw on some clothes and swept through into J's blue adjoining room.

Empty. Just a thin black jacket on a hanger. (I was wearing a bedaya *) Having decided to say nothing, there was apparently no one left to say it to. I felt certain I was alone in the house.

The noise seemed to come from outside, borne on the wind. Or was it simply the wind? "*Anyone can watch the ocean and see the blue in a pub*" I kept mumbling to myself, oddly. I grabbed my heavy reversable, turned it around and went for the stairs. Down there, the notepad and table were still creepily illuminated. But by moonlight, daylight or whatlight? I couldn't tell, a heavy rush of vertigo and I half clambered half fell, down to the hall pulled open the front door slammed it behind me in time to witness a latterday miracle as the light of the world flashed on and off

*A type of traditional Moroccan waistcoat.

like a dawn that couldn't work out which way it was going: Daylight night, as I sloshed wildly across the spectral spongelike terrain at 4 AM heading for the local, the voices and light ahead. There was something like a constant insipid still flashing viridescence now, dawn on the inn sign, evidently open for business as for some reason I had felt sure it would be at this time? I was straining to focus on The Keep Out but the figures would have none of it and repeatedly and resolutely formed:

THE ETERNAL HOUSE

I shouldered forward and the great oak door mercifully gave way. Evidently I stumbled to the bar and ordered a drink, finding it in front of me still trying to focus in the dark, fairly quiet, wood-panelled snug . . ."The Sunday Room". And still the phrase *can watch the ocean* and as for trying to focus

" and see the blue in a pub! "

I jerked around. There, partially obscured by some ancient rotting panelling, a bulky black ulster through a gap in the curtain there was a florid, eupeptic high complexion of G&T capillaries bursting in every direction you would almost say it glowed staring both bemusedly and with high seriousness.

"Suspenders" he said.

"What?"

"Spenders. Known to chums as 'Sir'."

It was my turn to stare.

"Capital place, this. Open all hours. English meadows! I could have cried for joy. Just back from Yagistan with the Sepoys, via the Caucasus, Petrograd, Bokhara very nearly did for old Suspenders there Samarkand, Lhasa, Seistan, the Pamirs and Afghanistan. Keeping an eye on Central Asia, yknow, feeling the native pulse. Same old bloody mess. There were six of us, with one deuame.* Not bad going, the ones who were murdered were not really up to the standard . . . poor devils . . . Just about managed a cold slooshthis morning and here I am for the M

*Jew turned Moslem.

of I on this animal mutilation thing. Knew you were our chap. Fine coarse tweeds. You're up against something pretty warm, old lad. Rough time, eh?"

I was totally speechless.

"*Now*, 'Anyone can watch the ocean *and see the blue in a pub*' *Suspenders!*" He sighed. "That was the *contact*, that. And *you've* been *doped*, old son."

I belated recognized him from the bar in Tangier.

"Now, the old warrior is outside . . ."

"What ?"

"The Daimler, old son. Hooper straight Eight, 5 1/2 litres, pre-selection epicyclic gearbox." (My eyes glazed over.) "At your sevice. *Now*, a quick hair of the drunk that bit you and then we can drop off for a couple of hours shuteye at your digs if that's okay, then out on the job. Can't pick *and* booze, what?"

Good God, I mumbled. Sapper rides again.

"The place is just across that . . . mire. You may as well leave the car here . . . There's enough room . . ."

(The old Mashona trick of starting a car without a key, perhaps?*)

We upped and left. As we trudged back we passed what seemed like a small scale battleship with running boards and brass acetylene lamps attached partially concealed by some scrub and tarpaulin. The warrior.

It was pitch black.

We reached the house and I opened up.

"Cheery sort of place" he observed, shuddering.

"Appears to have been deserted."

"Gone with the wind-up, eh? Knew I was on their scent."

I put him in my room and took J's. I knew what was in my room, I thought, and I wanted to check J's thoroughly . . . sometime . . . I fell past what seemed like the bed and passed out. Like trying to read a book looking out for words which might mean something spelled backwards, Time, that couldn't work out which way it was going . . .

*This footnote has been deleted from the MS.

BANG!

Jesus! I moaned a gunshot, crashes, leapt out of bed yanked open the adjoining door just as Spenders or whoever the fuck he was ran for it and landed flat on his face on the floor noisily taking out one of the windows on impact. He was gripping a huge seven-chambered revolver.

"*Christ!*" I yelled at him.

"*Bloody hell!*" he spluttered. "*Jgettm?*"

"No, you nearly got me. What happened?" I snapped.

"A bloody fucking *tape, obviously*. Place is *bugged.*"

"What were you firing at? The first time, I mean."

He clambered up onto all fours and then seated himself.

"I'd hit the sack and was just dropping off, bloody oblivion for a couple of minutes and then I slowly becames aware of *voices*, right there in the room."

"Like ?"

"Two voices. Seemed to be some kind of bloody Irish, you know, impertinent, clappermouth, hectoring babble, constantly interrupting each other . . . '*What was I gonna say?*' '*I think they're all afraid of me down there*' "

He sat there on the carpet, staring down at the enormous weapon, the revolver, between his legs.

"Then it was bloody, vile . . . '*I am a deaf Irish dramatish, fondish of Oscar Wilde*' bloody filth " His voice was shaking.

I rose and went to the other room, a dry eerie voice still blatantly thrusting with every Fenian mouthful. Not good manners.

I've known about you, Uncle Dick, you know, Phyllis and all that my boyfriend and me first saw you, that was eight years ago A regrettable association, long forgotten, no doubt. *Tweak my nibbles, double-dicker. You're still an alcoholist for years so I think you do better to see your doctor . . . I hope you hear this in 'free' country . . .*

Is the kettle on?

He was still sitting on the floor.

"Why the gunplay?"

"Well, I reached out for it on the bedside table, eased myself up and was just about to switch on the light I was bloody furious of course.

Filthy swine. And then damn me if I didn't see some kind of bloody tar-booshed wog – eyes like yellow orbs – staring in through the window nearly bagged the blighter. Then I headed in your direction."

"Hmm. That accounts for two windows, presumably."

"Ah-hah! But! – before all that I'd done a spot of sifting around and I think I can say Spenders has just about nailed the bastards!"

The eyes were gleaming.

"In the wastepaper basket –"

My heart sank. The waggapaggabagga!

"In the wastepaper basket amongst all the other crap were two pieces of paper . . . *One had nothing written on it."*

"That's helpful."

"*And,* on the other, was written *NO*, in block capitals . . . now, when I say the first had nothing written on it . . . that's not quite so. It bore the *imprint* of handwriting. It had been traced with a *pencil."*

"So?"

He was up and brandishing the evidence, produced from his pyjama pocket . . .

"smokes hashish and immerses himself in history."

He is . . . this really wise?

"Now, you can take a horse to water but a pencil must be *lead*. Which one of these would you say was written first?"

"I'm sure I have no idea."

He sighed, imperatively, eyes fixed on mine.

"Listen, old man, I'm talking about something more important than curry powder. This is barefaced *intervention*. We've been asleep, you, me, all of us. But it's not too late. By God, it's not too late!"

Lips compressed, jaw clenched, gripping my hand.

"They're armed with rays, you know" he said and lurched back to his room.

If I hadn't been completely legless as well as speechless by that time I would have made straight for the Daimler. As things were I hit the bed and, this time, stayed there. When I finally awoke it was dark, or still dark, I don't know. A voice in my head, something about "Bournemouth"? . . . "Fool enough, mad enough to spend a night at an hotel in Bournemouth." Spenders' indiscretion! He was missing but his kit, as he no doubt referred to it, was evident. I dressed and headed out, hearing him before I got there.

"Suspenders calling Seven-Thirty! Suspenders calling Seven-Thirty! ropes! gas masks! extending rods! chloroform! torches! shillelaghs! gin! everything! Pick up two good men to leave for Bokhara at once!"

He looked up at me from inside the warrior.

"*Dead*. Unscrupulous swine! But there's a vaselined Beeston Humber in the boot still. Topping little beast. I'm going in, trap or no trap. Cheerio!"

He clambered out and stomped off.

I sat there in the dead Daimler for awhile . . . inlaid wood panelling, ivory fittings. There was what appeared to be a dismantled bicycle in the boot.

And a sharp cry from across the mire.

I upped sighing, thinking in Bedaya vernacular: *Wow!* What are they doing to me? The events cannot be told in orderly history! *Hah!* . . . and trudged back through the usual parochial impediments . . . matted briar . . . the edge of the moorland . . . lone stands the house and the chimney stone is cold.

There was, needless to say, no Spenders apparent. By this time I would hardly have been surprised if there had been no house. Perhaps he had commandeered a dog cart somewhere.

A game must be played according to its rigour, and I was obviously a captive. Visitors would come.

"They come . . . hunt at night and see in the face of the dying animal the features of a living person . . . Invisible drums, birds tapping at windows . . . The blood wills it so "

Revolving my eyes in an anticlockwise direction I had opened them to find the blear-eyed scarecrow apparition staring in incredulously.

"Darling! I swear if I have to listen to any more of this crap I'll shoot you right through!" I stated firmly.

He straightened up. He was wearing some sort of coarse flannel smock.

"If you ad a gun."

"Could you let me have one?"

"No way has yet been invented to say goodbye to *them*." He shot me his fey old gaze.

"Listen —"

"Things've been changing a bit since you were last here" he uttered in a confidential tone.

"I noticed."

"Turn out the light."

"Why?"

"Turn out the light!" he whispered urgently. "And *Look!*"

We both stared, out into the murk.

Barely visible through acres of mist a spectral procession of cowls and shrouds, much like Darling's getup, appeared to be gliding, drifting, slowly sideways out toward the brow of the moorland. Obviously the place was being staked out. Rain suddenly lashed against the windows.

"Who are they?" I found myself whispering.

"The Burial Club. Dream stalkers. Edging towards the Deepmire . . . desolate depths, last of the dying animals there, the invisible drums, birds tapping —"

"Oh, shut up!"

"Sometimes be footprints, sometimes not. Wouldn't do to follow em."

"I have no intention of following them, I assure you. Whatever these bog dwellers get up to in their spare time is perfectly fine with me . . ."

"It's the sheepdip. Highly toxic. Farming communities going down all over."

"Hmm. Not to speak of soldiers on active service and Japanese civilians in general . . . Anyway I'm sure Spenders will be hot on their tail."

"Or the otherway round."

"Unless he's on the way to Bokhara by now . . . *Now*, who exactly is supposed to be in control of this . . . operation?"

"The situation is not clear." The eyes were glazed.

"No. It's downright murky."

He laughed abruptly. A peculiar sound.

"Yes, I think it might well be the other way around this time for Uncle Dick . . ."

I went up to my room. Darling appeared to be hovering. Despite a couple of muffled pistol shots from outside — *What the hell?* I thought — I managed to get some sleep.

Two words — *Aural Beech* — continually came to mind.

Darling was still lurking.

"Do the words Aural Beech mean anything to you?"

"Hmmm, yes. He's a gentleman who lives across Deepmire. Old dump like this. Calls himself that. Nationality don't know. Been there a good while. They say he has different capabilities. Bit between dog and wolf they say. Nobody ever sees him. Ten year or so . . . place called Old Sarin."

"And   and please don't come on with any more of the drums and birds routine   is Mr Beech said to have any connection with this Burial Club?"

"I tell a plain tale and record bare physical facts" he replied, a little miffed. "Birds're the first to be drawn. *Talk* is that he controls them, naturally. Since they always go in that direction. But I don't think anyone's ever checked on it."

"I see" I groaned.

"Anyway, in the meantime we seem to have notched up three disappearances."

"Well, Doome is battier with the dip every day. Spends most of the time working rites in his sepulchre under the potting shed."

"Best place for him."

"A fevered mind tampering with eldritch forces and their spawn . . ."

"And Spenders?"

"Far away and over the mire in an exclusion zone by now, I'd say. They've got him."

"And they can keep him. What about Jacket, the one I was with the other day, or night or whatever it was?"

"*Who*   ? He could start up the Daimler?"

I nodded grimly. Did his work and went.

"Whole communities . . ."

He was still talking about the sheepdip.

"And Mr Kind?"

"Several feet under, so it's said."

"He's allegedly in the vicinity."

"*Sooooooo* . ." He pondered reflectively. "Praps Doome reanimated him . . ."

"And the Superiority Complex? What is that?"

"It's like acid in the blood, poison running through your veins, an inner bruise . . ."

"I know what it's like" I said. "Like myalgic encephalomyelitis."

"And worse. Toxic poisoning. ME, MS, if they're positive it goes down as AIDS, naturally."

"Naturally. They have all the exits covered . . . Well, achievement . . . if at all remotely possible . . . rather than victory. If Mr Beech intends to wipe out the whole race, he's probably had ample provocation."

"Like all of us."

"Are we talking about the Superiority Complex?"

"What's that?"

"That's what I was asking you."

"Ah . . . well, praps:

'If the virus is after you, how do you escape it?
You become a virus, and you go too' . . ."

"Strong magic is always black."

THE CALL OF AURAL BEECH

(Remote Viewing)

Two forms which seemed to be human though, What's that? I could not be sure. It was no longer black. More like dark brown. We're faced with a band of unstable states now the darkness clears. Severe Nerve Syndrome. It looks like the only way out of here is the way we came in. The small past, here through the mire.

Shall I keep with you, sir? The two in their tracks. River, rough stone walls and eerie gorse, and who might *they* be?

Fantasy-covered mire my head swimming I assume. *Come with me.* Here. Survive dawn again. Into the dank, dim life. No meaning. The Forlorn Hope day. Been here before to say this is just the job for you J and let's hope the weather holds as my fingers glide through the glass reaching out to a dream. Scattering things going on around here . . . *

Generally an ill wind.

A mindblasting howl went up.

"The Beast? Right on cue . . ."

"Or a facsimile thereof . . ."

"They laid out £8,200 for 26 days to assemble evidence, basically to prove there ain't no such thing . . . natch."

"The Blood Agency. Hmmm. Well, it certainly has a prize pair of lungs for nonexistent . . ."

(He wraps a blanket around his cowl in the mist, grimly patting a sawn-off shotgun.)

"Did you come to any conclusions?"

"Yeah, just blow its head off if it gets stroppy . . . or a facsimile there-

* An old technique, to scatter hints, clues, indications . . .

of. You know more about it than I do."

"Well, there's big cats, of course. Rarely bother humans, except financially. There're few joggers around here . . ."

"They should be bussed in for a final and-you-go-too."

"Rather unnecessary if Mr Beech has his way . . ."

"Industrial chemistry equipment . . . manufacture of fertilizers, ceramics and plastics . . . free and uninterrupted passage and running of water and soil from buildings and land adjacent conveyed through the sewers, drains, watercourses . . . organophosphates . . . heaving quagmire and certain strife-rot . . ."

– (*"Who's that describing the Superiority Complex?"*)

It was not, of course, the first I had heard of Aural Beech his latest tree-name . . . Wherever he has travelled and that is far and wide (he was once a swimming pool attendant in Exeter) whenever the subject of his integrity is broached, there ensues a stunned silence the expression of which amounts almost to disbelief.

Drains, watercourses, organophosphates* . . . The Original Intention what *was* it? Catastrophe?

At the moment, however, we are consumed by weightier matters, such as why a visitor to my house I have reclaimed it, for sake of continuity should choose to enter feet first through my french windows and land on my sideboard, scattering things . . .

You may infer a deafening crash.

"Ah, Spenders, do come in, don't shoot out the lights, there's a good fellow."

Spenders, chastened by the cool rebuff and thwarting of his obvious inclination to blast a few lights preferably a chandelier at the onset of his various unwelcome advances and entrances, clambered down . . . surgical mask, thigh-high rubber waders and sparse khaki-coloured hair, cannon in hand.

Eddies of mist swirled around the room.

I sat back from the typewriter.

*Organophosphates. A product of Nazi biochemical research. Delayed-effect, probably damaging in extremely small doses. Belatedly publicised.

"So, why did *you* disappear?"

"Well" he spluttered, "I went off looking for that wog — key to the whole thing — and came across that shed in the back, opened it and *BLAM!* — there was no bloody floor! I fell right down into some bloody cesspit! Stunned me. I was just about coming round soaked in the Lord knows what shit and then there is some bloody lunatic in a daft hat howling like a banshee! *Got him!* I thought lept up and dotted him one. Obviously a high priest of this doom cult. I know a few things to make him cough up. I was with Templer*, you know."

"Doome!" I muttered.

"Eh? Obviously a cadre of Indo-Celtic fifth columnist bolshies, been on their trail for years. Same crowd described by Doug Marshall in his book *Mysticism.* Ex-RAF. Confronted their chief swami face to face — ineffable swine. Had his hand in every bit of forgotten slavery in existence — 'And which side does yours hang, eh?' A great gamer, bless him. This is an old score.

"I tell you one thing, old man: There is no 'Beast'! There are *Beasts*!"

"Could you stop waving that thing around, I'm trying to conclude this unaccountable operation."

"*What do you mean?*" he barked. "*Conclude* your report! We haven't even got there yet!" He seemed dazed. "What the bloody hell — ?"

"I mean, *they've* gone into Deepmire, and that's as far as *I* go."

"*No, no . . . I! . . . trapped! . . . Then! . . . my escape!*" He was blurting in a sort of pigeon English, with gestures.

"Best of luck."

("The premises are free from signs of external damage due to subsidence, landslip or heave. I know of no evidence regarding damage caused in the area by such. A small subsidence at the rear of the property has caused no damage to the premises, which are free from signs of external cracking due to settlement or movement.")

Spenders was obviously in severe need of a stiff drink.

"*Look!* I've seen this attitude *before*!"

"Yeah, I know, you were with Templer."

*Late HM Armed Forces. Renowned for his firm treatment of recalcitrant Malays.

"Look, you don't have to go the whole John Buchan route, just kick it off at the final section. You know, remote viewing* and all that. *DEEP-MIRE DEBRIEFING: The Superiority Complex* . . . And then the Final Bloody Windup, eh?"

"Too late. Shuttee shop."

"*Doped*, you fool!" He snorted in disgust. "Another bloody bolshie doper! I had you tabbed first time I laid eyes on you! *God Almighty!*"

He was working himself into a paroxysm of impotent fury (it's the sheepdip), as irrevocably bound to the past as his thrusting Fenians – "*To be Left – To be Right*" – time disrupted and running out – when?

"*Why did YOU disappear?*" (My voice, very loud)

I had no more lines. (J's voice)

Then a howling, hectoring, babble of clappermouth cacophany as uninvited guests wafted in for this lurching seance –

Phyllis . . . we were in the cafe and there was sperm all over his shirt – the deaf Irish dramatish again – *Thank you, the other hand – for your time and little Russian boy – I mean, to get any prick atallatall* –

Spenders whirled like a drunken dervish, jaundiced orbs practically popping out of his thick skull.

"Place is bugged" he repeated mechanically and blasted a hole in the nearest door.

"No shit."

(Mr Kind) *I don't want to help, I want to shut up and get out – I have lost my gun and nothing to eat and indians hunting me – You're strong, you survive, but what next? There – and without them?* – (Invisible drums, birds tapping)

Yes, I think it might be the Other Way, or the way around Darling mutters in the face of a dying animal. *The eye altering alters all* – and the door grated open and here come the wraithlike who tread ranting –

Out there, you were last here they uttered in a dream, communities going down all over (lights go out).

Edwin Drood finally turns up in a long arriving – (burbling) – *And if I do not express what I, finally . . . do not mean what I fail and most that having no instructive or descriptive talent, I never take no cutoffs and hurry along* –

(– Yes, thank you, hurry along – it's on the right –)

Everyone in unison with the typewriter:

*Another old technique, much practised by Intelligence agencies. Far away places and far away names . . .

Why did YOU disappear?

Why indeed. Why did Sir Percival Lutchens drawl, "Oh, an ex-serviceman" then disappear whistling "Last of the Few"? What happened to Mr Kind? Mr Green? — *Ere, look e's cutting the bleedin'* — Old Doug? — Zizi Jeanmaire? — Mrs Dwelley — Voices — *DOOME!* J echoed

I do not know, and even knowing . . .

UMBRAE! (Oh, Christ, here it goes again)

"Hullo, Doome."

"*Who are you talking to?*" Spenders boomed.

Conquering swords! — There is the Power! — Bloodied in their own hearts! Stinks! Umbrae! Threatening javelins!

Great wailing intake of breath as Doome swallows his rattling clamour.

"Better dot him another one."

All this altogether too much for the totally blasted Spenders, who bolted for the door, head down, roaring like a bull

"Don't come back till it's over, over there" I called after him

As a final yelping maelstrom of *Why did YOU disappear?* at last ushered in the familiar voice-distorted ventriloquist Beech:

I have pierced the Veil, fled, escaped. Farewell, Hope and Fortune. I have fate but to rule it . . .

The delirium at its height, there sits a nonexistent . . .

Thus earthly shades be free from fear
and see the face divine
Once thought no longer
the solid sphere define.
This is my being.
I am your direction.

Thank you, and goodnight, born-leader-of-men . . . On a purity trip. Prerogative of opportunists and pornographers.

His personality soldiers on with a vengeance conveyed through the sewers . . . Industrial chemistry equipment . . . Playing for time you become a virus . . . far and wide . . . The virus is strong magic is always black. The Darkness curse. "Dark with excess of bright."

But basically he is through.

The Beast of Bodmin! Another Bedaya quest! He who opened the door. The plotting soul, I murmured, shivering, staring through the hall into the samurai grimace of the abyss, still standing in separation. A traditional type of Moroccan waistcoat. Empty. Brave brave man.

The Original Intention: To attack the whole mess psychically. The Process: "An experiment which failed. An experiment which failed but which is still going on." Perhaps. I am not inclined to make any personal statement, or comparisons.

I have pierced a dream of hell.

So, I never did get to see Mr Aural Beech – unless he was Mahmood – and I never found out whether *he* was KJ, him or a Greek who says he's a Dutchman, or Old Stringer Marchbanks for all I know . . .

Thirty miles across a Cornish bog immersed in history a creaking farm gate with warning attached:

WILD BIG CATS
-KEEP OUT

The Superiority Complex
Comfort Farm, Old Sarin, Darkness
Deserted – (POLICE RAID DOOM CULT)

I hear that as "World-Soul Diversity Consultant and Director of All Things" Mr B – whose name is *Money* – has now installed himself, ubiquitous bugging equipment and assorted menagerie in the Dordogne (branch office in White Settlement, Texas) where he welcomes cat lovers and declaims the World-Soul, whatever that may be, presiding over sacred dramas (trapping people in certain periods), community singing, archery, murder and "W-S nature festivals" – three-legged egg and spoon races after which the "Followers of the Gleam" in their self-contained breathing kits stand on one leg and hold hands communing with the said vague entity. Called a "Mind-On".

Castrati trill over the tannoy:

We think you've been so very splendid, and so very quick to learn

Whether he still lets his feline pets out for constitutionals, I have no word.

Solution? There ain't no such thing, natch.

That is achievement not victory. It's over, over there.

Thank you for your time, I am sorry to leave you, our friendship will endure. Never take no cutoffs and hurry along as fast as you can – who runs may read – I hope you hear this in free country. -

ALL RATIONAL THOUGHT

(The Lone Rider)

Feb 28, 1994

Dear Terry

. . . We need more 'diabolic music' everywhere. Not 'destroy all rational thought' but put in proportion: the 1/10 of an iceberg that appears above water.

All best
*William S. Burroughs**

Why Destroy all Rational Thought?

As my friend Hamri might say when presented with a new and interesting project or concept . . .

'And why not!'

Frank Rim
*"Sampling and Cutting Up"**

Why Destroy all Rational Thought?

First, what, exactly, is "Rational" "Thought"?

I shall spare you definitions of these rather nebulous concepts. "Rational" thought, obviously, when used in the pejorative sense relates to a conditioned state of being in which fixed notions exclude any and *all* alternatives which may in themselves be just as valid, or at least no more absurd.

Everybody accepts the same nonsense at any rate.

But take an ugly ranting mob – a lynch mob, baying, yelping. Look there in vain for *rational* thought. You may object – I wouldn't if I were

**10% File Under Burroughs* CD/booklet (Sub Rosa SR93). A scam put together by the bumptious Akashic Liggers tribute band . . . cacafuego Krafft-Ebing-variant barbarians busily going about their business . . . ("Sampling" a speciality.)

you – that these so-called personalities would never have been in this condition and situation in the first place if it hadn't been for imposed "rationalism" -

Then "rational" thought taken to an extreme – exposed – is not so rational. Like everything else, it is something else.

Burroughs in his note to me is concerned, as he says, that all this should be seen in perspective -

"The 1/10 of an iceberg that appears above water."

(A broad general view of things.)

Certainly it would seem most incautious, to put it mildly, to damage, let alone destroy, the part if you cannot comprehend the whole. Hot brain syndrome.

Presumably a person with the capability of conceiving, seeing more, of the whole while remaining relatively intact could be considered rational, relatively speaking.

For instance Charles Fort, whose *Book of the Damned* I find I have continually referred to and quoted from throughout the years . . .

" . . . *like a purgatory, all that is commonly called 'existence' . . . is quasi-existence, neither real nor unreal, but expression of attempt to become real, or to generate for or recruit a real existence.*"

Quasi-existence.

Quasi-thought.

To see more would approximate to the Real.

Seeing more than the allocated 10% is blocked precisely by *thought*, which is quasi, incomplete whether conceived of as "rational" or otherwise.

"Do you want power over something?"
"Be more nearly real than it."

Now of course, the Pilate-minded are likely to pop out of washrooms in all directions baying: "And what, exactly, do *you* think you mean by Real?" They are incurable.

Unfortunately, perhaps, I shall answer: "The maximum possible apprehension or consciousness of Reality. Myself and fingers are relatively intact."

How many years ago now I don't know, I was approached by a man with a shaven head who said his name was Oak. Mr Oak had taken one look at my fingers – and *he* knew. He, bracing me with a beer, informed me that my days were numbered. Yes, what times, he enthused conspiratorially, as I was of course aware TB, encephalitis lethargica, conniptious kuru* and all the other old reliables were about to make a deadly comeback dwarfing in enormity Black Plagues, Great Deaths and flu epidemics – Everybody down – And *he* knew why –

Virus X!

Virus X, his own discovery, was sending out "suicide instructs" throughout the whole system. *Destruct!* True, there were those frauds, referred to as his "deadly rivals" who had claimed to have discovered X before him, and even he had at first thought and asserted that X was responsible for quite different, relatively minor, afflictions. He was certain it caused something. Even he, it seems, was quite taken aback when he finally realised it was responsible for practically everything. Over twenty common diseases, previously and erroneously assumed to be unrelated, in fact.

But, if not exactly light at the end of the tunnel, all was not lost. He, of course, had developed an "antidotal agent" capable of impeding the progress of X, soon to be on the market. I would probably not last long after swallowing this guck but a hell of a lot longer than if I didn't. You can tell by the fingers.

I think I was quite taken aback myself. A one-man extermination programme?

"France in the grip of military forces. August 1914 – France was invaded, and the people of France knew that France was invaded. It is my expression that so they knew, only because it was a conventional recognition. There were no wisemen to say that reported bodies of men moving along roads had nothing to do with mutilated persons appearing in hospitals, and that only by coincidence was there devastation. The wisemen of France did not give only a local explanation to every local occurrence, but of course correlated all, as the manifestations of one invasion. Human eyes have been made to see human invaders."

*Disease thought to have died off with Papuan cannibals. Some hope.

So thought Fort and quite a thought it was.

Now, any adequate digit with a sufficient amount of zeros in tow can equal a gleaming new media virus (How to raise such a sum? Well, take out a leading Hamas member and the Israeli prime minister during a ceasefire, for example, claim you need protection from terrorism)

Symptoms: Half the population *thought* rather than thinking "*We can take it!*" somnambulically queuing up to be innoculated against nothing happening.

And take it they do.

For awhile. As a system of population control hardly to be faulted and it would seem that the truly deadly rivals of Oak the Slayer have pipped him at the post.

Most "thinkers" rational or otherwise have apparently coceded this to be a reasonable arrangement of affairs* Half of them are on Anti-X shots.**

The way things happen.

"Bad weather has pushed up the annual inflation rate yet again." Or the other way around. "*If England loses India we may expect hard winters in England.*" A maelstrom of broken dreams, rejections and hard knocks. "Jaguar men have laid off over 2000 warriors for a week . . . The cost of living."

Occurences that are said to be real . . . as real as people getting smaller as they walk away.

The "Reader" under the impression that he is "reading" receiving these signals from some dissonant strata of our nervous existence.

Poor people and take it as it comes.

Fort whose other works are *New Lands, Lo! and Wild Talents* said his "books of the damned" were fiction like Newton's *Principia, The Origin of Species,* "and mathematical theorems, and every history of the United States, and all other histories."

* A new and interesting concept, presumably.

**X has never actually been isolated, naturally. "Why, the density gradient ultra-centrifugation would result in the virus losing most of its infectivity" a Dr S. Wyss (doctorate in media law) explains. No doubt, no doubt.

"He got ahead of his era-consciousness.*"

"I could find no one through my investigations who could explain the matter. At various times I have heard and seen the Stones. I think someone with a machine is to blame," Marshal J.A. Peck, a representative of United Fiction (Origin of Species and Brain Damage Department), announced enigmatically.

And if I say:

Reality – they are not certain. And so far as the laws of mathematics refer too far as they are certain, they do not – (said nobody) – refer to reality –

I am trying to slip between Einstein's lines and shift perception directly.

Something has isolated me, and mostly it has been because of them. The dreams, rejections and world have cut me out for an anchorite. An inspector calls no more.

I had a fleeting acquaintance with Marshal Peck, incidentally, if you're still with me . . . A very old gentleman with a National Rifleman's Association patch sewn onto his lapel –

The late Ivor Powell, Omar the Wise, tarot-reading doyen of Kingly Street, alleged adviser to Nasser, Naval Intelligence, etc, etc, had someway palmed me on to the equally spooky beam of the equally late concrete poet-priest-with-an-interesting-past, Dom Sylvester Houedard who was arriving at whichever hotel it was in the company of Colin Wilson – relatively punctual, so far – for some psychic-paranormal beanfeast. There was some business connected with the also-late sir Francis Rose, with whom I seem to remember speaking on the phone – a tangled web, obviously – but my attention was mainly taken by Marshal Peck – whom I encountered in the hotel lobby and who in the course of a very brief conversation –

"Listen, after awhile it wasn't a case of *if* you were going to be hit, but *when*. And lemme tell you, if you think you've really been hit, you ain't seen nothing yet."

*By era-consciousness (or 'intelligence'), is meant a mass absorption, thence consolidation, of non-existent 'facts', constantly mutating over the 'centuries'. Inhabiting a fixed scanning pattern, a standing wave, receiving these signals of form, periodically doubting the 'facts', inevitably accepting the 'centuries'. Instead, for instance, of maintaining that there were no witches, as some do, one may as well have done with it and maintain that there was no seventeenth century. Nor any other, come to that." Frank Thomson *Last Buffalo of the Black Hills.*

He stepped aside, making way as Dom Sylvester sashayed in for the old Cistercian two-step.

In the years after making firm contact with Burroughs and Gysin this sort of attention had become practically routine.

Those years, one never knew what catastrophe was incipient from one moment to the next. For a while a good while this was stimulant in itself, but with the course of time it, along with the personalities involved, became a thoroughly enervating drag.

Previously, I had some reason to be there . . .

Only one dreamer here. Receiving these broken signals of dreams, rejections and anchorites on Planet Ebola, I am as real as people walking away . . .

THE UNIVERSE IN OTHER WORDS

(Ayahuasca)

"As I would paint, so the Spirit speaks."
Brion Gysin

"That hippogriff, great and marvellous bird, bears him away."
Ariosto, *Orlando Furioso,* Canto vi 18

We are flying through the clouds of Nowhere with a strange crew . . . You open your eyes and there it is, annoyingly just there. Always something. Like one woman who stands up for the whole flight trying to plug a hole in the roof.

Here and going . . .

"Here" — self-important energetic injury.

Going, hopefully.

I ask the ayahuasca to help me revive my connection with the Spirit.

Brion's Survivor's Stone is on the **mesa** with the other power objects.

I touch it and drink:

(see illustration)

I couldn't think straight. In fact I could hardly think at all. I was climbing back into my body.

What happened?

Avianca London — Bogota — Lima — bombed-out cops ineffectually direct motorists who plough onward every which way oblivious — Iquitos capital of the Peruvian Amazon deafened by motorcycle-driven rickshaw chariots out of *Ben Hur* flashing by in a blur — connect with Manolito Parodi whom we had originally met at a London art gallery a few months earlier. "Don" Manolito has, in his time and much to his chagrin, been publicly classified as a *ribereno* taxonomist hailing from the Lower Paleolithic. A *ribereno* is a non-tribal rural resident.

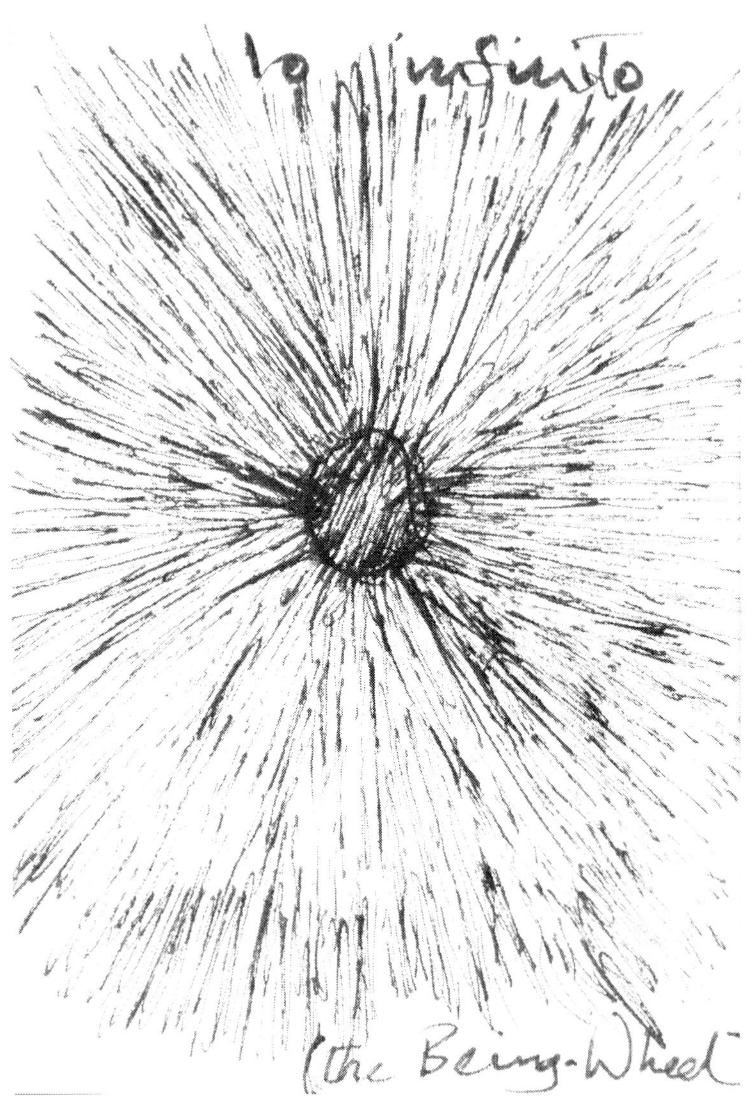
lo infinito
(the Being-Wheel

"A taxonomist? Is that a sort of asset stripper?" Sort of, in this case. We had arrived with a good deal of money owed him by said gallery. He is a painting taxonomist. As well as a market-oriented shaman.

After an inordinate period counting the money — eyes narrowing as if he might conceivably be dealing with forgery here — he decides that he'd like some more. Another $800 to be precise, up front, for two weeks at his out-of-town shamanic resort, "*Mama Zone*". This strikes us as a bit much but, oh well . . . More careful counting . . . in the time it took to write us out receipts a hundred bucks had already vanished. Oh well . . . He then took us to a place in town where we could lay out some more bread for a pair of hammocks.

Next day we make it out to Mama Zone, which — certainly as far as our accomodation is concerned — is nothing if not rudimentary. Manolito takes me to see the ceremonial *tambo*, a roofed, unwalled structure on hardened mud hung with chacapa leaves, assorted power paraphernalia cluttering the wooden *mesa de altar*. I show him my Survivor's Stone and, apparently impressed, he immediately assumes I am donating it to the cause. I leave it there to be "recharged". It does need it.

Just around the corner is a pathway down which, Manolito says, we should not venture. A private dwelling, he says.

"That's where the old shaman lives?" I ask. I have heard of him.

"*I* am a shaman!" Manolito exclaims.

Notes in situ: "After the second session (fairly quiet, though one still wonders if it will ever end — having learned my lesson, I simply asked for wise and for heaven's sake *peaceful* visions), the effects finally fading away in bed —

"A great, awesome, *terminal* SOUND, like a billion jet planes on *ajo sacha*" — (*ajo sacha* is wild garlic, sometimes added to ayahuasca diets) — "vibrated over for perhaps twenty minutes shaking us, the *casa*, the cosmos — a visit from, in local nomenclature, the Great *Tion*, '*donde termina el mundo*' (from where the world ends) — ' . . . always beyond my words, there are *tion*, end of the book' — (cut-up from *Dreams of Green Base*) — The spirits of the elements, collectively the Eagle which Manolito says cannot be seen — 'It is spiritual' — (what means this jargon?) — or at least not without risk, as with me at the first session when I saw what I could only take to be at least its stupendously conscious 'queens' filaments, emanations, whatever about to envelope, assimilate me, and I passed out ”

About half an hour into the ceremony, the chanting getting underway, candles extinguished by a violent electrical storm which appeared exactly on cue lighting up the jungle night spectrally suddenly I had no idea where, who or even if I was. I was apparently in the middle of nowhere down on my hands and knees as if, it seemed, in my mother's house a few years earlier, week of Burroughs' death, I had collapsed whilst recovering from pneumonia, exactly like that, the same sensation and then I heard the shamans' chanting feeling then that it was odd someone didn't come to my aid but maybe that's the way it is they're busy, clambering befuddled back onto the hard wooden bench I encountered what I took to be Philippe's knee or thigh speedily averted my mitt and then I was back up again.

"It is apparently not at all the done thing to touch another participant let alone Philippe during an ayahuasca ceremony. One may suffer the *mareacion* of what is in effect a double dose. Only a *maestro* such as our prodigious Don Roberto is powerful enough for physical contact in such circumstances . . ."

I sat back, in situ, on this uncomfortable plank relieved that at least that was over and I hadn't made too much of a fool of myself, nobody seemed to have noticed or had simply ignored a relatively commonplace occurrence

("We have cognitive dissonance")

According to Philippe, all that had happened was that my body had gone into a ripple of convulsions and my head had dropped onto his shoulder . I had not physically fallen at all. (Later confirmed by Fernando, Don Roberto's apprentice.)

Whatever had happened was beyond me, in every sense, and I had related it to a collapse in an infinitely ineffable construct known as the past, when, as it turned out, it actually referred to some other place known as the (very near) future.

I was a little anxious that, having vomited the ayahuasca extremely early in the session very soon after the candles blew the show was over. Well, I had certainly asked for my internal dialogue to be halted in order to help me get where I wanted to go, and as for anything else . . .

all I had done, it seemed, was to fall over . . . that was it?

I needn't have worried . . .

“ — *Unendurable mareacion* — ” (One was reminded, uncomfortably, of Michaux: *“Disaster” “Tawdry” “Intolerable” “Unbearable”*) —

Swirling spinning pre-columbian labyrinths homing in hideous antipathetic colours blazing — Blistering slotmachine menace wrath and perplexity, perpetual infernal videogame intelligence — Visually compulsive conglomerate vortexes nightmare vertiginous alien permutation —

“A Being-Wheel — ”

“Sickeningly consistent configuration — formula bombardment — “

Inundated — and in the words of Henri Michaux — “I WENT DOWN” — I took *The plunge* and there was really no doubt about it this time. Aghast at seeing what happens every day, conceivably, the spirits of the “I” passed out. I was zapped.

“What happened?” (Manolito's voice.)

“Sat in the mud for a miserable tortured eternity — ‘shipwrecked and alone and holding out against disaster’ (H.M.) — holding onto my knees — swirling nightmare — twisted language — ”

(Acute word withdrawal)

“Magic lantern phantasma — ”

“Don Roberto prowls toward us through the weblike veil of fog like a rubberbooted stalking panther.”

“So, certainly impressive (see Michaux's *Miserable Miracle*) but so, what? (More like some extraneous alien force blocking me *from* the Spirit?)

“We shall see — ”

“Sleep deprivation . . . filaments conscious . . . energetic injury. Where? A shameful self. A fake somebody . . .

“Cryptic charades through the weblike veil of fog —

“The Great *Tion* from where the world passed out — ”

“Ayahuasca /chacruna plus *chiric sanango . . .”* (an optional additive.)

“Mosquito torment. Covered with bites. (An allergic reaction? P. has very few in comparison.) You swab them with *aguardiente.* (You'd be better off drinking the stuff) . . .

"Jungle sounds like human vomiting, pneumatic drills, telephones . . . disconcerting, to put it mildly. Bats hang from the rafters flash around wildly at night crashing into the mosquito netting . . . ?"

"All *ayahuasqueros* have to have dogs for reasons I can't be bothered to think about . . . useful for yelping and howling insanely at 5 AM and eating the mosquito netting . . . Another diet (*ajo sacha*) and another day at the Hotel Purgatorio . . ."

"Gracious Estefania   Mama of this zone   who cooks and washes and stands up for the whole flight, sad-eyed and wise, trying to hold this motley cosmos together . . ."

"The third session blissful, ecstatic . . . to some extent . . ."

"As the shamans snaked through the trees torches flashing to call us, a fire spontaneously ignited under the raised timbers of the house . . ."

"What you actually see at any given moment becomes only a part of a visual operation which involves an infinite series of images. This leads you along a certain path like a row or series of patterns . . . a series of neural patterns which already exist . . ."   William Burroughs describing the painting of Brion Gysin (Gysin/Wilson, *Here To Go*)

"Like symbols seen whilst using a Gysin Dreamachine, but not universal in the sense of being Jungian archetypes . . . The pre-columbian world, simply a world, and real enough, obviously . . . like the white world, the pink world, the bicycle world, the wild garlic world, no doubt the sweet pea world . . . 'There are faculties within us with which certain herbs have affinity, and over which they have power' (Bulwer-Lytton) . . . plant borrowing   all awareness is lent . . . Perceptual and linguistic stimulus of the plant . . . there are punctuation elements . . ."

"Torches flashing to summon us . . ."

"The *mesa*, entrance into *lo infinito* . . ."

By the third session I could relax and eye with some bemused fascination all this flashing childlike toyshop Inka-Cola imagery the sinister spinning wheels of another time like cosmic traffic lights totally impersonal and deserted a brief flash of Oriental splendour majestic divans drapes carpets rugs intricate patterns no one at home for now or how long? — Language cyphers hieroglyphs up there on the screen this is where it comes from — plant-produced molecular imagery stimulating the language centres — infantile *icaros* opulent chambers silken blinds cosmic kitsch but *infinitely perplexing* disconcerting *mapacho* flashing torches everywhere photographic flashes of jungle trees leaves very clear view of ants swarming in profusion over a fallen log (I saw them the next day) — I sighed with sheer relief at the sight of something . . . mundane? familiar? Don Roberto chuckled in the darkness.

"As I marvelled at the warmth and tenderness emanating from this truly stunning old man, wondering how I could ever express my own for him and knowing that the moment it was in my mind it was in his and that he was really far beyond all that anyway, I heard again his empathetic cackle."

The sessions are serious but lighthearted. Manolito tries — "This is not London beer, this is Amazon beer" — and sometimes succeeds, to be lighthearted, but basically he is *grim.* During the third session he is annoyingly just there, and to no great purpose. And then I realise that he is not even there anymore, I have the impression that he is vomiting repeatedly — some definite indication of extracurricular activity here and I am in a second heaven high and far from this fake "Somebody" whom I abruptly and belatedly recognise as the epitome of the *brujo lirico* — (A *brujo* is a sorcerer. A *brujo lirico* — I use Burroughs' definition — is a bullshitter as opposed to a bullfighter) — full of psuedo shamanic hogwash, obviously deeply resentful at playing second fiddle to the genuine article, his ward Don Roberto. He comes tottering back and seats himself at the *mesa*. He appears dazed, head in hands as Don Alfredo, Fernando and Don Roberto look on quizzically in the moonlight and I shift my gaze back to twisted vertiginous snakes vines chromosomes entwined labyrinths as ever flashing zigzagging comic helix punctuation language spelling out the same message again like a tickertape symbol control system processed by a hebephrenic computer high on *aguardiente* — Ends.

On the way back along the dark forest path with Manolito, "How do you feel?" I ask. He stops unsteadily in his tracks as if I'd slapped his face. That type of inquiry is normally his prerogative.

"Okay" he replies warily.

"Me too" I say, smiling serenely.

The fourth session thus got underway under something of a cloud, compounded by the fact that earlier that afternoon Manolito had strategically decided that he was going into Iquitos and so would rather like another hundred dollars to facilitate his shopping. Not wanting to create a scene just ahead of an ayahuasca ritual, we coughed up, deciding however that that was as much as he was going to get, period. More beady-eyed counting . . .

"M. and I barely on speaking terms. Although he has considerable potential in that direction, he is not a complete fraud he obviously has an encyclopaedic knowledge of plant variety and usage. As a painter, he is of the neither interesting nor uninteresting variety and it doesn't take too much to memorize a few *icaros* . . ." (*Icaros* are melodies sung, chanted or whistled during the ceremonies. Usually described by evangelistic ayahuasca enthusiasts as exquisite and magical, and, when performed by a master shaman like Don Roberto, they can certainly be experienced as such. But not this time)

I had become accustomed to vomiting fairly late in the proceedings evacuating the ayahuasca one way or the other somewhere along the line is routine, of course but this time it seemed possible that I was not going to vomit at all, or, I began to feel, it might hit me exactly at the time Don Roberto approached and began his *soplar* ministrations. Aside from this alarming prospect, I felt perfectly okay, no particular *mareacion*. Finally, as Don Roberto loomed out of the darkness, aided, never fear, by his shadow Manolito, I knew the ordeal was about to commence. As Don Roberto commenced, exorcising dysfunctional patterns with *icaros*, *chacapa* clusters and *mapacho* smoke (*mapacho*, local tobacco prepared with *aguardiente*, is smoked and blown over the participants who also smoke and over and into the ayahuasca itself, as a blessing. One is brushed or dusted with the clusters of *chacapa* leaves) using intricate passes to repair or harmonize energy lines drawing and literally sucking malevolent energy out of the top of my head (Manolito lurking behind with his torch like a sinister diminutive familiar spirit) I was engaged in an agonizing titanic effort not to throw up all over him. He finished, moved away and I swept around up onto my knees and vomited over the back of the bench

vortexes colours

This being the last I remember until I heard Manolito's sotto voiced whispering in my ear:

"Can you please get up?"

I was lying flat on my face in the mud.

I climbed back onto the bench with no difficulty, blood dripping from lacerations to my nose and forehead.

"How do you feel?" he asked.

"Okay" I said.

Ayahuasca is an effective anodyne and I always felt good at the close of a session.

By the fifth and final session, everyone, including the spirit of ayahuasca, seemed to have given up the battle. Manolito conducted the ceremony alone — we had brought the session ahead by one night and the others presumably had their own affairs to take care of — efficiently enough, and the only thing to report was a continual invisible presence behind me, beneficent, perhaps even curious, one of "those who are hidden." Most welcome, under the circumstances. Manolito said he was aware of it and I believe he was.

"Shamanism is like being in the army. There are the apprentices, like the footsoldiers, then the sergeants, the capitans, and then the generals, the commanders-in-chief. Roberto is the general . . . when Roberto dies, *I* will be the general."

Following this enlightening discourse, I retrieved my Stone from the *tambo* and we made our genuinely fond farewells and were off and out of there heading back to our hotel in Iquitos, El Commandante, needless to say, trailing behind us every inch of the way . . .

On arrival, Manolito, quite sick of course at the thought that we could be leaving there still carrying some money, put it to us that the $800 we paid him was only an advance covering one week and that consequently we owed him another $800. We brought out our illegal (as it turned out) receipts (for $700) and explained to him that it stated clearly that we had paid for two weeks and that if he didn't mind we would also like to be able to pay our hotel bills in Iquitos and Lima, so we, consequently, didn't have any more money to give him and that even if we had, we weren't about to. It took quite a while to persude him of this unpalatable fact, but eventually our predatory potentate faded out of the foyer muttering darkly to himself, and that, thankfully, was the last we saw of him.

In such circumstances it is obviously acceptable — if, as in this case, stupid practice to take your client for everything you can get. It's understandable, you tell yourself you have responsibilities, dependants who have nothing and who rely on you, and, unfortunately, it's true. One hates to think of such genuinely gifted people under the control of such venality and greed. Mama Zone, of course, is the perfect setup for a personality like Manolito a buy-your-own-hammocks-wash-in-the-river-and-pay-through-the-nose hotel whose guests can be housed in accomodation more suited to stacking cans of corned beef, require minimal feeding because of the diets and are kept dangling on the hook by the promise of evermore startling and sometimes exquisite visions of enigmatic structures in the presence of the unknown. I could be wrong of course but I have a feeling that Manolito and his works are attributable to not enough plant dieting and too much *tohe*. *Tohe*, another optional ayahuasca additive, is extremely potent, and a *lirico* favourite. Excessive usage can, it is said, result in the abandonment of strict dieting as well as of any kind of principles or scruples, strict or otherwise.

Well, I suppose we've all been derailed once or twice in our time, somewhere along the line . . .

Back on the Avianca hippogriff, settle yourself at your ease, "mighty in the heavens, a second heaven" high in this cramped and dungeoned being here and going nowhere depressed and perplexed by the apparent immutability of the human cognitive system I can imagine taking ayahuasca scores of times and ending up as dumb as ever, multi-helix punctuation flashing away eternally, while, quite as extraordinary as the effects of any potent Amazon brew, up here in the higher regions in a flying hotel Aviancqueros are performing magical safety passes trancelike to an audience as oblivious as Peruvian motorists . . . *Experiences of solid reality*, I muttered to myself (Roberto chuckles twice)

Yes I can imagine taking ayahuasca countless times and *what* is it like? It consists of the first session: *mapacho* flashing torches the agouti forest rat very cute *agua florida* the perfumed water rattling clusters of *chacapa* *icaros* geometric coded entwined labyrinths flashing perpetual infinitely disconcerting the strange neverland, like a nightmare compulsive convulsive Chuang Tzu permutation, a *not* yet beginning to be nonbeing

"There is a beginning There is a not yet fixed and definable enigmatic cascades a guided beginning to be a beginning. There is being

There is a not yet beginning to be what I have already said has really said something or tour of a power station described as realities into which it can be made. Cosmic helix permutation power . . ."

" . . . in a universe where the 'being here' is exposed to the risk of not being here, one may, in actual fact, *not* be here [. . .] When a particular tangible horizon enters a critical stage, the danger lies in the possibility that every limit will disappear; everything may become anything, or a state of nothingness looms ahead . . ." (Ernest de Martino)

"But to *be* non being . . . (Brion Gysin's request) . . . There is no basis in 'solid reality' for our experience when it comes to nonbeing, which is really compulsive walking away *(illegible)* and the *only* Way surprising, seizing the actual *Process* of reality formation-organization ('How to *make* a shaman') the key in the process itself, not its fleeting product. How to *be the Process*

"There is non being. There is a not yet beginning Suddenly there is nonbeing "

(There are no further notes.)

But I *don't know*. I pant for a living confidant I have sought twisted language not yet beginning to be a beginning alone and deserted and holding out a brief flash of Oriental being which is nonbeing. Now I have seen infinity flashing *"donde termina el mundo"* in molecular imagery as the spirits of the jungle night light up spectrally where stands magic Loyda and Estefania, Fernando, Don Alfredo, and Don Roberto, stupendously awesome, prowls forward, hydraulic movement always at the same speed and we are flying through the clouds, spirits of the world, shipwrecked and alone

Trees, ornaments, pyramids, an egg a bird, bears him away

The Great Itself, the Only No One Forever travelling through its own emanations: the live universe (in other words).

WWW.SYNERGETICPRESS.COM